ALWAYS OBEY ORDERS: THE
F.V.W. MASON FOREIGN LEGION
STORIES OMNIBUS, VOLUME 2

ALWAYS OBEY ORDERS

THE F.V.W. MASON FOREIGN LEGION STORIES OMNIBUS, VOLUME 2

F.V.W. MASON

ILLUSTRATED BY
SAMUEL CAHAN

COVER BY
PAUL STAHR

POPULAR PUBLICATIONS · 2023

TABLE OF CONTENTS

ALWAYS OBEY ORDERS

Because the family motto had always been "Obey orders," Major Mike Lockheed was defending the ford against his own brother, who had been sent back to Mexico by Napoleon III

1

RETREAT

"NO TWO WAYS about it, Spurr, we've got to get that ammunition back," panted Major Mike Lockheed, turning a red and dusty face over his tarnished silver epaulette. Then he peered ahead again, his long, red-uniformed body swaying easily to his charger's powerful gallop.

"Yep." A bronze-featured rider who, in a faded brown uniform, was riding a horse's length behind, nodded vigorously. "We shore got to get it back, or them Frenchies will just nacherally massacree us if we try to hold them fords."

Major Mike Lockheed, the foremost horseman, looked very young and lithe in his dusty and spotted red uniform; but his strong features were set, and he kept his singularly clear blue eyes thoughtfully fixed on a lazy pillar of dust that arose from the hot, sunlit plain perhaps a half mile ahead. When he peered back over his broad left shoulder again, he found that he could see the first view of his sixty-odd Jalisco lancers very clearly. Further back, the whirling dust only permitted glimpses of tossing manes, flaring red nostrils, the shimmer of helmets and the quick flick and snap of the yellow and red pennons on the tips of long yellow-shafted lances.

"Wish to hell we hadn't split forces, sir," growled the leathery faced rider galloping at Mike's elbow. "We'll be

The long lances were dipping and stabbing.

onto these here *mal hombres* in two shakes now, and they'll outnumber us quite a heap."

"Zapatos and Ribera are better off out of the way, Lieutenant Spurr." And at the mention of the names, the young commander's features darkened momentarily. Then he called out over the clatter of hoofs: "Think they'll stand?"

Beneath the visor of a tall felt shako set on the head of Lieutenant Spurr, ex-sergeant of the Second United States Dragoons, narrow black eyes studied the billowing dust ahead.

"Reckon so, sir; with them pack loads of ammunition, them guerrillas can't keep up this speed much longer. But they's got nigh a hundred men and us less'n sixty. What'll you do if they try to stand us off?"

"We'll charge 'em like hell!" briefly returned the red-uniformed leader as he slowed his powerful golden bay to a gallop more nearly the average speed of the small, wiry mustangs ridden by the little red-and-yellow-clad lancers.

Pursuers and pursued were now pounding along over a

broad mesa where grass, burnt yellow-brown by the hot sun of Oaxaca, made a smooth, endless carpet. But the heavy golden brown dust was just as thick here as anywhere else. Straight toward a line of jagged blue mountains the marauders were retiring, followed by a cometlike trail of dust.

As the interval narrowed, Mike suddenly found himself wondering why el Hiena, that brutal scourge of Republicans and Imperialists alike, had sent such a small force to pounce upon the pack train of ammunition so vital for a defense of the fords of the San Gorgio.

The dust in the air grew steadily thicker, and soon the sweating pursuers thundered past an abandoned pack horse, which limped feebly along, lathered from crest to fetlock; then a second and a third.

"They'll stop soon," Spurr cried.

Slowly, Mike Lockheed reined in his horse and motioned back the foremost of his followers. Better to close up his ranks before charging upon these savage marauders. He glanced back again, saw his men riding in to form a loose triple rank, their lance points twinkling in the sun and their helmet-shaded faces eager and tensed.

Good soldiers. Yes, old Colonel Lockheed, his father, had been right. Mexicans, when properly led, made as good cavalry as any in the world. In fact they were quite a likeable people when a fellow got to know them the way he and Andy had, since their father's return to Mexico after that unhappy war between the two republics.

GRIM PLEASURE FILLED him as he beheld the fugitive guerrillas flogging the pack horses in a last and vain effort to urge more speed out of them. One of the bandits, a huge fellow in a towering sombrero and a brilliant green sash, suddenly drew rein and began waving his arms, signalling certain of his followers to the rear, while the pack horses kept up their lumbering flight.

As he perceived the bandits' preparation for battle, Mike's breath began to come shorter. With a grim smile, he loosened and drew from its scabbard the heavy American saber that was securely tucked beneath his left knee.

Blinking in the swirling, sun-lit dust, he beheld Spurr, looking like nothing so much as a fierce old eagle. He was directing the lancers to close in, and Mike felt a sudden lifting surge of joy—here was war at its best. A level field, a strong horse between his knees, good men at his back, and a vital mission to perform. For get that ammunition he must, before the momentarily-expected soldiers of Napoleon III came bearing down to attack the tactically vital fords of the San Gorgio.

Amid the dusty haze ahead, he could distinguish certain shadowy forms, where el Hiena's rear guard was forming for a stand. He glimpsed two or three varieties of uniforms

which lent credence to the rumor that this bold and ferocious bandit mob was being daily strengthened by deserters from the Republican as well as the Imperial and the
French forces.

Fierce delight filled Mike's heart. Rising in his stirrups he turned, and with his saber swung in a glittering
arc, signalled his men to form line. Quickly, the tireless
lancer mustangs galloped out to either flank, a few strides
behind those of the big, whiskered sergeants who spurred
to the front, their red-crested brass helmets gleaming in
the bright hot sun of Lower Mexico.

The young major's blue eyes flickered ahead again. Ha!
El Hiena's rear guard was forming up fast.—Better get
going before they were well set. Lord, but there were a
lot of them over yonder, and they looked as though they
intended to keep the ammunition at all costs! That made
it interesting, since he also intended to have it at all costs.
The defense of the fords was on his shoulders, and on a
successful defense of the fords depended the security of
General Benito Juarez's whole army.

"Going to be one hell of a good ruckus in a minute,"
yelled Spurr, above the jangle of equipment and the trample of many hoofs. "Wish your brother Andy was here.—
He'd like this."

MIKE, BAREHEADED AND looking very big and powerful
on his golden bay, nodded vigorously as he raised the saber
again and filled his lungs.

"Ready-y-y!" His voice rang out like the peal of a war
trumpet; and amid a mad flutter of pennons, sixty-odd
lancers swept to the horizontal, as in a single motion. In
their saddles the brown-faced, black-haired Republican

cavalrymen settled themselves more solidly behind their lance butts.

"Ch-a-a-rge!" Mike's saber flashed downward. The *encurados*—so called because at one time Mexican lancers had worn leather breast plates—were now in a compact line. They spurred their mounts and raised a long drawn yell of *"Viva la Republica!"*

Forward they raced, each man low in his saddle, like a jockey, and carrying his blue-white spear point well out in front. Off to the left, Lieutenant Sarolla, in direct command of the Jaliscans, was yelling like mad. He had lost his helmet, and his long blue-black hair was snapping in the air like a sable war flag amid the red horsehair crests of his men.

"Hi-yah! Yah! Yah!" Mike leaned low over his saddle pommel, just as his father had taught him, extended the long saber to full reach, and then touched his thoroughbred's flanks with his spurs. Outraged, el Aquila gathered his powerful quarters under him and sped forward, heading towards the center of that dense, vari-colored throng ahead.

"Hi-yah!" Again Mike's voice, much deeper than that of any Mexican, yelled out the old Second Dragoon war cry. El Aquila's hoofs were drumming madly now over the hard, yellow-brown earth, eating up the space like magic. Behind, the lancers were cheering with their thin, womanish voices.

Closer, closer! He could see the bandits advancing to meet the charge. Some were pulling out machetes and swords, some were unslinging carbines, and a few had lances—a motley array if ever there was one. But the guerrillas were even more numerous than he had imagined; Mike realized that with a sudden sense of apprehension.

FIFTY YARDS, TEN yards. Deliberately, Mike singled out a big, black-bearded bandit who rode out in front. The rascal was still clad in a bedraggled green and yellow uniform— he was evidently a deserter from the Imperial Hussars. As old Colonel Lockheed had taught him, Mike aimed his saber point at the deserter's hairy throat, and set his whole weight behind the weapon. Black Beard saw him coming, read his intent, and levelled a huge pistol, reining aside his powerful black horse as he did so.

Two heart beats more, and that black bearded face, all yelling mouth and staring eyes, materialized just beyond el Aquila's pointed ears. The deserter's pistol cracked as loud as the report of a field piece, and something stirred Mike's red-yellow hair. Then, a brief fraction of an instant later, came a hoarse scream and a jarring, rending impact on his sword arm.

As one receives an impression during a flash of lightning, Mike sensed, rather than saw, the marauder's green-uniformed body bending far back over his saddle cantle, saw the black beard tilt skyward. Then he flipped over his wrist, knuckles uppermost, so as to allow his charger's impetus to clear the saber point. With surprising speed, the saddle of the snorting black was emptied.

Hardly had Mike returned his saber to the "on guard" position when el Aquila carried him headlong into the bandit ranks. There, a yellow-faced mulatto in a dirtied orange velvet bolero aimed a vicious slash at him with a machete. Barely in time, the young major's saber parried. Then Mike, rising in his stirrups, slashed in return, and felt his blade bite deep into the mulatto's yellow neck. Scream-ing like a slaughtered hog, the guerrilla slipped sidewise in his saddle, and was lost to sight in the press of conflict.

The hot, bright air quivered with sound. From the corners of his eyes, Mike had glimpses of pistols flash-ing, of horses rearing, backing and snapping at each other. With deadly accuracy, the long Jalisco lances were dipping and stabbing; and Mike, raging through the guerrilla ranks like a young Mars, heard one or two lances break as falling bodies snapped the stout pine shafts.

It was a very busy three minutes that followed. Then, with astonishing suddenness, the fight was over. But to Mike, all seemed confusion, noise—and above all, dust. Through a shifting, choking pall he could see sprawled bodies, abandoned weapons, shadowy riderless horses that galloped about, their eyes and nostrils wide with fright. A wounded bandit was squatting in the dust, rocking from side to side as he clutched his bloody head and shrieked, *"Dios! Dios! Dios!"*

Panting, thirst-tortured and sweat-bathed, Mike watched a squad of lancers engaged in running down the handful of guerrillas who had vainly sought safety in flight.

Like yellow hawks, the *encurados* swooped down on their prey. Now their yellow-and-red bodies gathered behind the lance butts as they braced for that powerful surge which would pierce the luckless guerrillas between the shoulder blades; and now came the thrust that sent them reeling out of the saddle, to roll over and over on the dusty brown grass.

"How—we fixed?" Mike gasped when Spurr cantered

up through the dust haze, busily wiping his reddened saber blade on the mane of his horse.

"We ain't lost more than five or six, sir," he reported, and rubbed the dust and sweat from his forehead onto his red cuffs. "We sure gave them guerrillas a nice lacing."

"*Seguro.*" Mike grinned and beckoned his bugler. "Have the men form up, we'll resume the chase and have that damned ammunition back inside of fifteen minutes."

BUT IT IS well known that "man proposes and God disposes." Even as the triumphant lancers came trotting back to the rallying point, carefully picking their way over the fallen, tumbled bodies of their late enemies, Mike's restless blue eyes suddenly ceased their habitual inspection of the horizon. He stiffened in his brass-mounted saddle, as though one of the lancers had jabbed him.

"Great God, Spurr, look at that!" he cried, flinging out his arm to the left.

The veteran officer in brown whirled about and rapped out a string of curses. "It's the Frenchies—God help us!"

With the glazed eyes of despair, Major Mike Lockheed watched a column of horsemen trot out from the shelter of a steep arroyo off to the left. The prevailing colors of their uniforms were blue, gold and green; no room for hope that these men on the flank might be friendly.

"Yes," jerked Mike, reining in el Aquila. "French and Imperial lancers. Got to git, to save our necks.—Oh, *damn* the luck!"

As he watched the strange horsemen appear he realized, with a pang of despair, that victory had been snatched from his fingers. To continue to pursue the stolen ammunition would be to invite the complete annihilation of his force and himself. Characteristically, he lost not an instant in handling the bewildered little lancers.

"*Son los Imperialistas!* Ride for your lives! *Aprisa!* Back to the fords!" Slow-witted, the dusty *encurados* in yellow and red stared in incredulous amazement at this new foe who came charging forward as soon as they had spied their enemies, in a long, glittering column. Behind these appeared an even larger mass of infantry in uniforms of blue, red and white, and the latter immediately began to deploy with a skill that commanded the respect of Spurr, that hardened veteran of the Texan and Mexican wars.

"Real *soldados* over there," he yelled as he stopped to catch a loose horse for a dismounted lancer.

"*Andamos!*—Hurry!" Mike urged in furious Spanish.

At last aware of their acute peril, the dusty *encurados* wheeled their mustangs. With many a frightened look over their shoulders, they bent low in their saddles to spur back in the direction from which they had come.

Cursing with disappointment and apprehension, Mike lingered on the scene of his recent triumph until the last man had begun his flight.

"Pick a straight course!" he called to Lieutenant Sarolla as that wild-eyed officer went racing by. "Try to—make the fords."

"*Sí,*" replied the Mexican, and galloped on, his right hand busy with the quirt. "But I—afraid—few of us—get there."

BITTERNESS WELLED LIKE an acid spring into Mike's heart. Hell! The ammunition was now irreparably lost, and defeat loomed large on the horizon. For, as the thorough-bred bounded along, he foresaw how completely impossible it would be to hold the fords of the San Gorgio with the scanty supply of ammunition his men now possessed. Yet his orders had been that the fords must be held.

It wouldn't have been so bad, he told himself, if he could have been certain of one or two of his officers; but a number of things which had happened recently gave ground for bitter reflection. For instance, how could el Hiena have known by which route the ammunition was coming into the San Gorgio country? There were a dozen trails and roads, yet he had unerringly ambushed the right one.—There was a traitor somewhere, of course.

A hoarse shout from the rear lashed his thoughts back to the troubles of the present. He glanced backwards and smothered a bitter curse. Lord, how quickly those green uniformed lancers were coming up! Theirs were fresher horses of course. There must be at least a hundred of them, behind those blue-clad French officers.

Back past the deserted pack horses pounded the desperate chase.—Sarolla led the retreat, and Mike, gloomy-eyed, reined el Aquila in to the pace of the slowest *encurado.*

Just as a group of bare, treeless hills rose from among flat little prairies that reflected the sun's heat like mirrors, the first casualty occurred. The horse of an *encurado* put its foot into a hole and fell heavily, knocking its rider senseless.

"Poor devil!" thought Mike as he galloped past the struggling horse and the inert lancer. Too bad there was no time to save him, but the enemy were now not over two hundred yards behind. He *must not* get captured or killed, he must get back to his forces on the San Gorgio. Zapatos, Ribera and the rest never could be trusted to obey orders and hold the fords.

AHEAD OF HIM he saw the fleeing *encurados* strung out in a long line, the strongest horses far in the lead, heading for that row of low, green hills which marked the course of the San Gorgio river. How familiar it all was. Mike found it strange to be fleeing for life through that same countryside where he and Andy had spent their late boyhood.

Damn! Tragedy was near at hand, for just ahead of him an *encurado* on a failing horse was thrashing the poor animal with the butt of his pistol in a desperate effort to keep up with the others. No use, the mustang's sweaty legs were wavering with fatigue and his hoofs landed with heavy, lifeless thuds. Mike caught a glimpse of a flat, brown face turning despairingly to the rear. Too well the lancer knew his fate if he fell into the hands of General Méjia's troopers.

Mike shouted to the *encurado* to pull up, but just as he did so a shot rang out, and the lancer pitched head foremost from the saddle. Only wounded, the yellow-clad fugitive staggered to his feet and started to limp off; but a pair of hussars in green veered from the main pursuit and quickly cut down the screaming wretch, in cold blood.

Mike ground his teeth in impotent fury, then reined in his charger, in spite of el Aquila's furious protests. When a gorgeous hussar sergeant came galloping up, swinging his curved sword, Mike turned and sent a pistol ball through the fellow's body. A touch of the spur, and el Aquila bounded away again, amid the furious yells of the pursuers.

"That evens the score a little," he told himself.

Only thirty-odd of the original sixty remained by the time the harried lancers dashed into a little valley where a rutted road wound between two high green hills.

"Now—our turn," Mike gasped to himself, and heaved a sigh of relief when a sudden volley from a dense clump of mesquite emptied a dozen of the hussar saddles to the rear.

Around wheeled the Imperialists, and dashed out of range amid a clatter of musket shots, leaving the hot earth littered with dead.

"First round's over," yelled Spurr, his black eyes watching the hussars' retreat to their main body. "All even—"

"Even, hell!" Mike was thoroughly alarmed. "What the devil are we going to use for ammunition?" He tried to conceal his anxiety, however, when three or four infantry officers ran up, among them his favorite subaltern, Roberto Escandón, a handsome young lieutenant of the *caçadores*, or Mexican light infantry of the time.

"*Qué hay?*" called the foremost officers. "Where is the ammunition?"

Briefly Mike described the disastrous end to the chase.

"Then all is lost, *señor comandante!*" declared a grizzled veteran of many a revolution. "We have not thirty rounds for each man. We must retreat before the French attack."

"Silence!" Trenchant as a saber was Mike Lockheed's command. "I'm giving the orders—understand, Captain Montojo? We'll not retreat until we get orders."

"Then may the Virgin take pity on us!" was the *caçadore* officer's bitter comment.

2

BROTHERS

FROM HIS BED, Colonel Frederick Lockheed, late of the Second United States Dragoons, and now a prosperous cattle rancher, raised inquisitive steel gray eyes when his tall younger son stalked into the room. The ex-soldier was gray-haired and there were blue-black circles under his piercing eyes. A man of sixty-five cannot suffer a broken leg and three broken ribs without showing it.

"Well, Michael," snapped the master of Las Estrellas as he struggled up on one elbow, wheezing with the pain of the effort, "did you get back the ammunition?"

At the foot of the handsomely carved four-poster bed, Mike paused and shook his dusty head.

"No, sir. The French came in on our flank just as we cut up el Hiena's rear guard. We had to ride hell for leather.—It's a hell of a war when they murder prisoners. There must be a gang of butchers over there—not soldiers!"

A bleak, reminiscent smile crossed the veteran's face. "War in Mexico never was played to rule—not since Cortez landed.—Well?"

"Looks like we'll have to give up the ford."

"You can't do that, Michael," said his father grimly.

"Remember the motto of our family, 'Always obey orders.' You've been ordered to hold that ford."

"Always obey orders." Mike wondered how many times he had heard his father say that—five or six thousand times at least.

"I only wish to hell you hadn't tried to ride that blasted mustang. I'm damned if I know what to do, Dad," he said, dropping wearily into a chair by the bedside. "Méjia's expedition is already here, and we've only thirty rounds per man."

The crippled veteran stirred impatiently, a pale shadow in the darkened room. "Yes, it's too bad, son. Especially since most of old Juarez's men are ready to quit. He's a game old cuss, and he deserves more help than he'll get. If the French don't set an emperor over Mexico, Benito Juarez will be the only one to thank for it. So you'll have to do your job somehow."

"What am I going to do?" Mike repeated, weary eyes on his father's sunken features.

"Use your head," advised Colonel Lockheed. "It's by using our heads that we Lockheeds have made good soldiers ever since America was settled."

"Where's Carolina?" Mike peered about the shadowy bedroom. "Thought she was here."

"She was, but she went out for some medicine and to have a talk with the foreman of her ranch. Naturally, he's terrified of what the French will do if they cross the San Gorgio." The old man's craggy features hardened. "Of course I didn't tell her they'll loot and burn Los Flamencos as thoroughly as they will Las Estrellas."

The young officer's reddish head lifted sharply and his sunburnt lips grew tight.

"Well, they won't burn either of them as long as I'm alive. We'll defend those fords to the last man."

Colonel Lockheed chuckled. "That's better. I only wish Andrew was here. Why the devil did you boys have to go fall in love with the same girl?"

MIKE SHRUGGED AND blinked, momentarily shutting out the wide bed, the glimmering candle and his father's pain-lined brown features. How clearly he could visualize Andy; lithe as a puma and handsome as a Roman centurion. How distinctly he could hear his brother's voice saying, "Now, look here, Mike, we both love Carolina, and it doesn't help matters that she can't make up her mind which one of us she wants. I want her so badly I know I'll get to hate you, maybe try to kill you, if I stay. We've been too close for that, Mike."

How Andy's sensitive gray eyes had shone with suffering. Mike could hear himself replying, "I feel just the same way, Andy.—What are we going to do about it?"

"One of us has got to clear out," the elder brother had said. "Then Carolina can marry the other—"

With surprising quickness the situation had been solved.

"Look there," Andy had said, pointing to a goldfish which lay drowsing beneath a lily pad in a little pool which occupied the center of the patio at Las Estrellas, "I reckon that fish will move pretty soon. If he goes to the right, I'll go away. If he goes to the left, you go."

And so they had stood there a long ten minutes, nerves brittle and eyes fixed on that gleaming little fish. At length, having spied a succulent fly which had fallen into the water, the fish gave a brief flip of its tail, thereby changing the destinies of three human lives by darting off to the right.

"So long, Bud. Be good to Carolina—she—she—" Suddenly Andy had held out his hand with a smile that had wrung the younger brother's heart. "Reckon I'd best be saddlin' up. See you in 'bout five years, maybe—Name one of 'em after Uncle Andy—won't you?"

"Surest thing you know, Bud!"

And then tall and handsome Brother Andy had quietly saddled up and loped off, to be swiftly lost among the purple-red sunset shadows of the rugged Oaxaca hills.

But Mike and Carolina had not named any children after Uncle Andy, for the very good reason that, not being married, they had no children.

In the hallway outside the bedroom sounded the resonant tramp of cavalry boots, and some one rapped softly on the carved door panel behind Mike.

"*Qué hay?*" he called.

"Captain Ribera, *Señor Comandante,* wishes to report that the French have sent a flag of truce. Their commander was brought here blindfolded and wishes to speak with you."

Mike looked up suddenly, and his shadow cast by the candle on the table by the bedside mimicked him.

"Very well," he called. "I will see him in a few minutes."

"Yes, talk to the Frenchman," advised the old man. "But be careful—those French are the best soldiers in Europe. Be careful, and use your head—it's your only chance."

"I'll try, sir. I—I want to save you and Carolina if I can. These French are said to be merciless." Mike nodded once, then he gently closed the bedroom door.

IN THE MAIN living room of Las Estrellas he found Captains Ribera, Zapatos and Martinez, those officers of his who had just returned from their fruitless search for the guerrillas along the left bank of the San Gorgio.

In the sunlit interior, the dark-featured officers seemed very ill at ease. They were staring fixedly at a huge, sunburned and bearded N.C.O. in a blue and red uniform, with crossed belts of white. He stood stiffly erect, just inside the front door of the ranch house. A red topped *képi* was clutched in his gauntleted right hand, and in the other a white flag knotted to a tree branch.

"Where is the commander?" Mike inquired of Spurr as he strode forward, his tarnished silver epaulets on a level with the eyes of his dark-faced staff officers.

"He's on his way," replied the gaunt Texan who alone approached Mike in size. Even as he spoke, a sentinel outside the door challenged with a hoarse *"Quién es?"* Voices muttered briefly, then the door latch clicked and an officer appeared in the doorway. So tall as nearly to fill the door frame, he was clad in a heavy blue uniform, on the breast of which glittered a single row of bright gold buttons. His collar was red trimmed with green, and gold epaulets rode broad, powerful shoulders.

Ex-Sergeant Spurr uttered a whistling gasp of surprise and stared as at a ghost. "God blast my eyes! Why—why, Mr. Andy, what in hell you doing in that French uniform?"

But the newcomer answered not a word. His sunburned, unshaven features, so strangely like those of the commander in red, were set in lines of iron as he stepped inside, eyes riveted on those of his brother.

With the stiff motions of a mechanical man, Andrew

Lockheed raised his hand in stiff salute, his bronzed face utterly devoid of expression. As in a daze, Mike beheld a sharp-faced and bespectacled French lieutenant who now appeared at Andy's left, follow suit.

With a conscious effort, Mike returned the salute while his eyes bored into the beloved features of that brother he had not seen in four years. Mechanically, he smiled and said:

"Buenas dias, señores, you may come in without fear. We of the Republican Army always respect the flag of truce."

IN THE BACKGROUND Ex-Sergeant Spurr stood very still, surveying the scene with mingled emotions. He alone, of the glittering group in that low-ceiled room, fully appreciated the deep tragedy of the situation. He, as few others, knew of that inflexible code under which Colonel Lockheed had brought up his sons.

"Thank you, sir," gravely replied he in the dust-spotted blue uniform. "I am Captain Lockheed, commanding the third company of the First Regiment of the Imperial Foreign Legion; and I have the honor to bear a message for the officer commanding such troops as may be guarding the fords of San Gorgio."

Making a brief bow, Mike replied, "I am Major Lockheed, sir; and I have the honor to command the troops you mention."

The grim farce continued, and Spurr's jet eyes were stony when the man in the green-trimmed blue uniform bowed again and said stiffly, "Permit me, sir, to present my lieutenant—André La Marche."

"I am deeply honored, *monsieur le commandant,*" quoth the lieutenant.

"And I, also," supplemented Mike with a mirthless smile. "This is Jake Spurr, my aide, late of the Second United States Dragoons, and provisional lieutenant in the Republican Army."

Mike found it hard to think, let alone to speak. Inside his head whirled a maelstrom of thoughts and emotions, which churned and seethed like working yeast. Campaigning against the French Imperial Army was one thing, but fighting a force led by his beloved brother was quite another.

How queer Andy looked in that heavy blue uniform with his gold buttons, green trimmings, rakish red-topped *képi,* and dusty, high cavalry boots. He was as lean and sunburnt as of yore, and there was the same reckless light playing at the back of those clear, gray-blue eyes. But about the mouth Mike noted some new and bitter lines, lines that might have been caused by long, lonely nights spent beneath foreign skies; lines that might have been caused by longings for a girl whom he thought to be forever lost. And Mike was aware that Andy was studying him no less curiously; no doubt finding him unfamiliar in this war-stained and theatrically gaudy red cavalry uniform.

"Well," Mike said suddenly, "please set yourselves at ease. And please forgive our having blindfolded you. I didn't want to miss the opportunity for a very pleasant little skirmish, which might have been the case had you been overawed by our numbers," he added with the ghost of a smile.

"We are delighted, *monsieur le commandant,*" said Lieutenant La Marche. "Le Captaine Lockheed has been telling me something of this beautiful country. I believe he has spent some time here." The sunburnt and powerful

Frenchman twirled a little brown moustache, and from behind his gleaming glasses shot a shrewd sidewise glance at Mike, as though to hint that he could be counted upon to carry out his part of this tragi-comedy.

STILL ANDREW GAVE no sign of recognition. He bowed briefly to Mike's staff, which, hurriedly dusted off, stood gazing with undisguised curiosity at these self-assured and coolly superior foreigners.

"Well, Captain Lockheed, we await your message," stated Mike, standing very straight by the desk which for four years had been locked upon Andy's private papers.

"Merely this," said Andy in a loud and penetrating voice, "General Lorençez of the Imperial French Army has sent me to reestablish peace and order throughout the state of Oaxaca. Too long has Mexico been the victim of self-seeking politicians.—France has unwillingly decided, in the interests of humanity, to put a stop to this reign of lawlessness.

"I, as an officer of Napoleon III, have come to urge you to surrender peacefully the fords of San Gorgio. My column is well armed, and is accompanied by three troops of lancers; my legionaries are the best infantry in the Imperial Service—veterans who can outshoot, man for man, any troops in the world."

Andy was speaking, Mike noticed, with an earnestness which held something more than the anxiety of an officer who desired to carry out successfully his mission.

"At the first practicable moment," the officer in blue continued, "my column, aided by a strong force of cavalry, will advance upon and seize the ford of San Gorgio, according to orders." He paused, as though to give additional emphasis to his next words, then dropped his voice to a solemn pitch. "If we meet with opposition, even of the slightest, I have General Lorençez's direct orders to exterminate the enemy, to ravage the entire countryside and to execute"—his voice quivered a little "—*all rebel officers found under arms* and operating against the provisional government of President Miramon."

As the Legion officer's announcement was ended, cries of mingled astonishment, resentment and fear arose from the brown-faced officers grouped behind Mike Lockheed's stalwart red form. Undoubtedly, Andy's threat had gone home.

Mike realized that his task was made no easier thereby. Fumbling furiously in his mind, he bowed ironically to his brother—a jerky little bow—and swallowed hard. God above! Andy had practically said he was going to burn Las Estrellas and hang his own brother!

How queer he felt! The long, low room seemed to have become suffocatingly hot all of a sudden... What devilish irony that he and one of the three beings he most loved should be thus flung at each other in merciless combat. It did not seem to be his own voice that said:

"What, then, do you advise, Captain Lockheed?"

AGAIN THAT BURNING earnestness crept into the Legion officer's manner. "Either surrender your arms, or retire beyond the Texiaco range. In the latter case," he continued, an unspoken appeal in his wide-set eyes, "I swear that the country will remain unharmed; the *haciendas* will not be burnt and peace and order will be maintained under French administration until such time as your new emperor, Maximilian I, the Hapsburg prince, who is a younger brother of Franz Joseph of Austria-Hungary, reaches these shores. Then, when His Imperial Majesty is firmly installed, the troops of France will be withdrawn."

As Andy's voice fell silent, a babble of staccato Spanish burst out to one side. A half contemptuous smile spread over Lieutenant La Marche's thin, aristocratic countenance. Understanding Spanish well, he quickly sensed the eagerness of certain of Mike Lockheed's Juarista officers to avoid the conflict in the offing. Quite correctly, he assumed that many of these gayly uniformed *caballeros* owned ranches and *haciendas* in the immediate vicinity. Naturally, they thought first of their property.

For a moment, Mike stood in rigid, miserable silence. Then, clearing his voice, he said, "Sir, we thank you for your consideration and gallantry in warning us of your intent; but on the other hand, we hold orders from President-General Juarez to defend the fords of the San Gorgio to the end of our power. We are therefore"—he drew a deep breath—"determined to dispute the passage of the ford.—And since we seem to be at a stalemate, I suggest, Señor Capitán," he nodded to his brother, "that we retire to deliberate in private."

"Very well."

A deep stillness reigned in that crowded little whitewashed room while the brothers, the one in red and the other in dusty blue, pulled aside a blue-and-white hanging and stalked in grim silence through a door to the left.

3

OBEDIENCE

IT WAS NOT until the two stalwart commanding officers, so strangely alike and yet so unlike, stood in that familiar study decorated with the trophies of Colonel Lockheed's thirty years of army experience, that they unbent from their rigidly correct military manner. On the walls about them gleamed colorful Creek war bonnets, Seminole headdresses made of gorgeous egret plumes, sabers, helmets, pistols captured during the Texan war. But the two brothers saw none of these. Of equal height, they stood gazing at each other; then, without a word, they flung long, wiry arms about each other and hugged as they had when, as children, some adventure had separated them for a few days.

"Andy!" cried Mike. "You old son of a gun. Lord, I am glad to see you. I've been turning the *República* upside down, looking for you these last three years. Where in hell have you been?"

The other one sighed, and his gray eyes wandered beyond the curiously wrought iron bars of the window. "I wouldn't have come home for a while, Mike; but I suppose it's fate. When I joined the Foreign Legion in Algeria, who in hell would have thought it would be ordered to Mexico inside a couple of years?" Andy's eyes, a little grayer and less blue than Mike's, suddenly sought his brother's, and there paused in unspoken inquiry.

"Carolina is well—lovelier than ever," Mike said, and nervously fingered his tarnished silver belt.

"I'm very glad of that.—Are there—have you any children?"

"No," replied Mike somberly. "It—Well, it was a damned big mistake, your going away—"

"What—Then—" As though a bullet had struck him, Andrew Lockheed's long body stiffened beneath the dust-powdered blue uniform, and the heavy gold epaulets on his shoulders shimmered briefly. "She didn't—you aren't—?"

Solemnly, Mike shook his sunburnt red head. "It wasn't long after you'd vamoosed that Carolina and I became engaged; but somehow, things weren't quite right. Both of us felt it, and then poor Carolina realized that it was you she really loved—" Mike choked a little.

"Please go on," said Andy, in that peculiar monotone some men use under stress of great emotion.

Mike's weatherstained silver epaulets rose under a little shrug. "Well, we stalled for time—put off the wedding to give me time to hunt for you. I looked everywhere—even up in Texas and down in Honduras—until this blasted war broke out."

"Good old Mike!" murmured, the other, and his hand closed over Mike's. "You always were a good sport."

"But I didn't find you, of course. We're still officially engaged, otherwise Carolina's *padre* would have married her off to young Sandoval. You know—that smooth young *caballero* from the city. I tell you, Bud, it's been mighty hard finding excuses to postpone that wedding."

"Carolina!" In Andy's gaunt, deeply tanned face burned a feverish anxiety. "Carolina still free.—God, Mike, how I've hungered and thirsted for a sight of her these last four years! I used to lie out in the desert, back in Barbary, and wonder what you two were doing. It never occurred to me that you weren't hitched up long ago. I figured you'd have a herd of kids playing all over the house. Where—where is she?"

A RATHER GRIM smile lit Mike's features. "She's here, *soldado*, here nursing Dad. A mustang fell on the old *caballero* a couple of weeks ago, smashed his left leg and a couple of ribs."

"What! Carolina here at Las Estrellas? Good God, Mike, she's in danger here!—You should have sent her away."

"She wouldn't go; you know what she's like—a real thoroughbred. Besides, her *padre* moved their rancho down the San Gorgio, until it's only three kilometers below us, here on the plateau. He calls it Los Flamencos, now."

A heavy silence invaded the little library while on Andrew's sun-darkened face appeared an expression of anguish.

"Good God, Mike!" he muttered at last. "I'm in a hell of a fix.—As I've told you, I have orders to burn both Las Estrellas and Los Flamencos, and hang you and your officers, if I catch you."

"Well," remarked Mike, "I don't notice you taking that ford yet."

Andy's dark head snapped up and he looked a little

taken aback. "Mike! Surely you aren't fool enough to think you can hold that ford against me? Why, I have under my command two hundred picked men of the best troops in the world. Besides, I've two hundred troopers of the crack *fijo de Méjico* lancers."

Mike managed a confident laugh. "They aren't enough, Andy. My troops are veterans, too; and they'll fight to the last gasp. But aside from all this, whichever way the cat jumps we're in a bad way regarding each other. For you see, my orders are to hold this ford and to execute any French officers I capture, in retaliation for the orders you've been given."

"Look here," cried Andy hoarsely. "Can't we—can't we do something about this?—We can't carry out such orders. Let's both resign."

Mike slowly shook his reddish blond head, and his shadow mimicked him on the white plaster wall behind. "You wouldn't do it, and I wouldn't do it. We Lockheeds don't resign in the face of the enemy. Dad would disown us both if we did. Suppose we go in and see the old gentleman. Maybe he'll have a suggestion. It'll have to be a brief visit, Andy. Our respective officers will be wondering what the hell."

"Yes," agreed the older brother, "I've got to be getting back to my command."

THE SPURS ON the dusty boot heels of the brothers jingled softly on the red tile floor as they quit the library. Solemn of manner, they made their way to that spacious bedroom in which the grizzled ex-colonel of the Second United States Dragoons lay on his bed of pain. As his deep-set eyes beheld that second tall figure in the doorway, he struggled up on one elbow, then sank back with a stifled groan which prompted a tall young woman by his side to speak with gentle severity.

"*Tio Fréderico,* you must lie still. It is only Don Mike."

"No, no!" choked the old man. "Look!"

And then Carolina de Fonseca's slender, white-clad figure straightened.

"Andrew!" The exclamation was punctuated by the crash of a glass of medicine which fell from her hand to shatter itself on the antelope skin beneath her small feet. *"Madre de Dios!* It is not possible!"

She made a dramatic and unforgettable figure. Completely clad in white, though her dress was no whiter than her face, she stood gazing from enormous dark eyes at that powerful, soldierly figure filling the doorway.

"Andrew!" With a smothered cry she darted around the foot of the great bed, and an instant later Andrew Lockheed's dusty blue arms were about her and his hard, sunburned lips were pressing fierce, hungry kisses on the vivid softness of her mouth.

Mike stood to one side, gazing fixedly out of the bedroom window. Apparently he was absorbed in watching pigeons flutter from a dovecote across the patio, to drink at the edge of the fountain.

Suddenly Colonel Lockheed's voice broke in. "Mike, is that a French uniform your brother has on?"

"Yes, sir." Like a private replying to his colonel, Mike Lockheed straightened.

"Then what is he doing here?" demanded the old man, his parchment colored features set. "Since when has a Lockheed permitted an enemy to enter his quarters?"

"He came under the flag of truce, sir. We have been parleying. Since he was here, I saw no good reason why he shouldn't see you and Carolina."

It was then that Carolina sprang back, eyes wide with distress. *"Dios de Dios!* What is this?—A French uniform? You must take it off, Andrew! You must never go back— never leave me again. Ah, my heart's own—!"

Slowly, Andy's black head shook. "Sorry, darling, but we don't do things that way. In a few minutes I've got to go back across the river; and then I'll have to do my best to burn this rancho—and yours, too—if Mike and his men make the least attempt at resistance."

IT WAS TO Mike, standing very tall and glum, that the poor distracted girl now fluttered.

"Mike, Mike! You who are always so generous, so gentle, so *caballero,* surely you know that our poor *soldados* cannot stand against the French. You will order the retreat and so avoid this mad encounter—no?"

And now it was the younger brother's yellow-red head that shook in sharp negation.

"Impossible, little Carolina. I have my orders from President-General Juarez himself—the ford must be held at all costs."

"This is criminal, stupid, infamous!" There was the wail of a breaking heart in Carolina's voice; and more than anything that had yet transpired, it moved the two brothers. They turned in unspoken appeal to that powerful old figure outlined beneath, the bed sheets, and saw written there a reflection of the anguish which Carolina felt.

"Surely, Dad," began Andrew, "there must be some way?"

But the iron gray head shook. "Obey orders, my boy—

always obey orders. I'll not hold it against you if you take this rancho and burn it to the ground. You will only be doing what I've taught you since you were old enough to talk. All I can say is—" his voice broke a little "—all I can say is—that you must both do your duty as you see it."

"No! no! no!" Carolina flung herself upon Andy, winding white arms about his big chest and pressing her tear-stained cheek against the cold, glittering buttons there. "I will not let you go again. *Dios de Merced!* What if you were killed, now that you have come back to me? Retreat, Andrew! You must, I implore you! Why should you lay down your life to force the French emperor's rule on my people?"

With a bronzed hand that trembled a little, Andrew stroked Carolina's lustrous black hair. Then he lifted her chin and gazed a moment into her swimming eyes. *"Adios,* darling, I—I must be going."

It was then that Carolina gave a tired sigh and sagged limp in Andy's blue clad arms. Swiftly Andy roused himself, kissed the unconscious girl, and gave her over to Mike.

"Take care of her, Mike," he said in a strangely thick voice. "Get her out of the way. For, God help me, I—I am going to attack—as hard and as soon as I can."

He extended a bronzed right hand, first to the old knight on the bed, and next to his brother. Then, with a faint jangle of spurs, he executed an about-face and stalked from the room.

4

TRAITORS

FIVE YEARS OLDER did Mike Lockheed seem as the sun, before its almost meteoric disappearance from the sky, hovered for an instant above the sharp crags of Santa Lucrecia. The last rays, beating in through the library windows of Las Estrellas, lit the weary features of the little council of war. A home-made map, roughly drawn by Mike Lockheed but amazingly accurate, was being studied.

Bending over the red-uniformed commandant, Spurr and el Lobo, the Yaqui chieftain, followed the frayed point of the quill pen with which Mike was emphasizing his remarks. Curiously enough, there were no Mexican officers present; Mike had deemed it wiser to be discreet about his plans.

"Now," Mike was saying, "here's what seems most likely to happen. The French will have to camp dry, or retire five miles to get water. It's a cinch they won't dare come down to the ford to-night, for fear of being ambushed; and the cañon is too steep anywhere else. Andy—er—the French commandant knows this. Right now they are halted; but I'm sure they're short of water and must fall back. Don't tell this to the rest of our crowd. I want them to think— Hello, what's that?"

From outside had sounded the clank of *accoutrement* and the trampling of many horses.

"Reckon that'll be Zapatos and Ribera and the rest, back from their wild goose chase," remarked Spurr somberly. "Hope they ain't wore out the hosses."

"They'd better not have," said Mike briskly. "Go out and order 'em not to let their men unsaddle; we're pulling out for Conino at sundown."

"Conino?"

"What?" The mahogany-faced Texan veteran nearly swallowed his quid; and even the Yaqui looked up quickly, though otherwise he betrayed no amazement.

"What the hell!" Spurr cried.

"That will do, lieutenant," cut in the red-haired commander swiftly. "I know what our men can do—and what they can't do. The French force would simply massacre us, even if we had plenty of ammunition."

"*Bueno,*" grunted the Indian. "El Lobo will do as his brother commands. The Yaquis will be ready to ride at sundown."

"But, major," protested Spurr, "we could put up a good scrap maybe. It'll look bad—"

"Maybe it will," snapped Mike, "but I won't have my force annihilated. If we stood a ghost of a chance it'd be different—"

"But, but—" stammered the Texan, spreading horny hands in protest "—we got orders to hold this here ford."

"That's enough, lieutenant. Go out and transmit my orders."

Ex-Sergeant Spurr's narrow mouth shut with a click and a certain contemptuous gleam crept into his eyes, though his hand went up in salute. Then he whirled about, going through the door, his huge dragoon's saber clattering in its war-worn scabbard.

"My brother needs me no longer?" inquired the Yaqui chieftain.

"Not right now," said Mike somberly. "Go and wait for orders, Captain Lobo."

FIVE MINUTES LATER el Comandante Lockheed was announcing to the rest of his officers his determination to retreat.

"*Nombre de Dios!* But this is cowardly nonsense," angrily protested Zapatos, the captain of Jalisco lancers. "As we rode in, we saw the French turning back.—They are in full retreat."

"So much the better. They are probably going to report back to the main column," explained Mike quickly. "At present it may be they fear us. Later they may return with many cannon and reënforcements. That is why I am falling back on Conino. We must have more men, more ammunition. The fords are safe enough now."

"Ah, I see," commented Captain Ribera, and nodded his brass helmeted head thoughtfully. "But is it not unwise to leave the ford and these ranches unguarded? What of guerrillas and bandits? Does it not invite raid?"

"There is nothing to fear since el Hiena is in full flight, to the south. You yourself reported so. That is right, is it not?"

"*Pero sí.*" The burnished brass helmet nodded so that its scarlet horsehair crest stirred lazily. "The bandit, may God blacken his face, is far down the San Gorgio valley. There is nothing to fear from him."

"Then we march in half an hour. To your units, gentle-men."

It was a bad five minutes Mike had with his father when the old man heard that he was retreating.

"Afraid of old Boney's legionnaires, eh? Or is it Caro-lina's whimpering that's made you forget your duty? Get out of here, you cowardly hound!" the enraged old man roared. "Get out and stay out! If I could walk, I'd kick you out. If you think you're doing me a favor by retreating, you're not. I'd rather have a hundred ranches burnt than have one coward for a son. Get to hell out of here—and don't come back!"

Red faced and furious, Mike had endured the tongue lashing, well aware that the colonel's parade ground voice was carrying out into the shady patio where his officers were taking a farewell drink of that cool Madeira which was Colonel Lockheed's favorite beverage.

DUSK WAS SETTLING fast when the little Republi-can force turned their backs on the fords they had been ordered to hold at all costs and, leaving behind the hospi-table golden yellow lights of Las Estrellas, set off along a winding trail which led up to distant Conino. It was all very silently done, and save for the occasional snuffling of a horse or the faint jangle of its equipment, the maneuver was well carried out.

"Why do you remain in the rear?" Ribera called out when Mike pulled rein and halted to let pass the helmeted, red-clad dragoons who acted as rear guard. These gaud-ily uniformed men looked like so many hawk-headed monstrosities in the gloom as, hunched forward in their high saddles, they set their shoulders against the pounding of the heavy little carbines slung across their backs.

"Just want to see that no stragglers drop behind," Mike nodded affably. "Ride on, captain; and tell the lancers up ahead to increase the pace. If we're to get to Conino by dawn we'll have to keep up a four-kilometer walk."

"Why not send an orderly?" demanded Ribera, a little truculently. "I would rather keep an eye on my men, I am no messenger boy."

"Do as I say!—And you, lieutenant," Mike called to Escandón, "ride into the center of the column and see that this eternal jamming up is stopped, or some of the horses will get kicked and put out of action."

Accompanied only by his aide, the lean Texan called Spurr, Mike gradually dropped further and further to the rear, until a good half kilometer separated him from the last dragoons in the column. He was very alert now, for in a few minutes more the column would be among the rocky hills now looming black ahead. Once among them, there could be no turning off the trail.

"Come on," he said sharply to Spurr, "drop this damned sulkiness. I won't have it! Keep your eyes skinned—I'm expecting some fun in a minute—"

"Yes, sir," said ex-Sergeant Spurr, but his manner changed not at all.

"We'll halt here.—Now listen—"

The two horsemen stood in silence for perhaps five minutes. The clatter of hoofs in the distant column was growing fainter when all at once a solitary dragoon appeared, a black shape against the gray hillsides. He was proceeding cautiously and kept peering to the right and to the left.

"Shall I wing him, sir?" muttered Spurr, sliding his Winchester from its boot. "That hombre's a deserter."

"No," was Mike's astonishing reply. "Let him alone. I want him to get away—he's more than a deserter."

Each of the silent watchers gripped his horse's ear to prevent a possible neigh, and they hugged the shadow of a willow bush as the messenger of treachery drew nearer, letting his horse pick its own course. Not a hundred feet away the dragoon turned off the trail, spurred his mount and moved off to the south at a cautious trot.

"And there," murmured Mike, "goes Fate in the shape of a traitor. Blast his yellow soul to hell!—Keep that horse quiet!—We'll have to let this hombre get well away before we make a move. It'd spoil everything to let him suspect anything. When we rejoin the column, I want you to take the boys from the ranch and cover the head and the tail of the column. I'll give Captain Lobo orders that the Yaquis are to cover the flanks. No one is to leave the column from now on. Kill any one who tries it. *Any* one, understand?"

"Yessir," said Spurr, and grinned in the dark.

WHEN THE LITTLE force had been on the march a long two hours, Mike made his way to the "point" and peered about, obviously in search of land marks. Presently he turned his horse off the beaten track to Conino.

"*Qué hay?*" demanded the lancer captain. "This is not the way to Conino."

"It's a *new* way," explained Mike briefly. "Last fall, when I was antelope shooting, I discovered this new route. It will get us into Conino two hours sooner than the old way."

"I—I protest," hotly objected Ribera, who came galloping up. "You may lose your way. I insist that we follow the regular road!"

Mike straightened in his saddle. *"I'm* giving the orders here.—Get back to your post, sir!"

On through the darkness blundered the little column, until all at once it dawned upon even the densest of the *muchachos* in the column that they were not headed for Conino at all, but for some point, the secret of which lay concealed in the agile brain of Mike Lockheed alone.

Great was the astonishment, and perhaps disgust, of certain of those dark-featured officers who rode with Mike when, with the rising of a waning moon, they beheld in the empty distance that deep gorge, like the Grand Cañon, through which the Rio San Gorgio pursued its course. Presently they came to the very correct conclusion that Don Mike Lockheed had been leading them through the barren uplands in a wide circle, and that by a little brisk marching they could arrive back at the fords of the San Gorgio in a short half hour.

"Es loco. He is mad," the officers muttered angrily, and Captain Ribera's mahogany-hued features were furious in the shade of his helmet's visor. On the other hand, Lieutenant Spurr's frown had disappeared like dew before the sun, and at the corners of his rat trap of a mouth was the same admiring twist that had been there on the morning when, as a sergeant, he realized how cleverly old Colonel Lockheed had posted the Second Dragoons at Buena Vista.

Twice, during the hours that followed, did the watchful, panther-footed Yaquis who prowled on the outskirts of the encampment pull from the saddle certain ill-favored Mexicans. These, with masterly carelessness, had been caught in the act of straying away from the lightless bivouac. At such times, knives glimmered briefly; and after that the skulkers became quite still.

AT LAST, CAPTAIN RIBERA drew near the stone on which Mike sat, deep in thought, his eyes on the drowsing horses and the prone figures of his infantry. Mike noted that the dragoon captain's features were quivering by the eerie light of the moon.

"This is an insult, *señor comandante*," he growled. "Why have you made fools of us this way? Why have you posted those terrible savages on our flanks? One of them nearly knifed me just now!"

Mike heaved his long frame to its feet, a dangerously tight smile curving his lips.

"Well, my dear captain, I'm sorry that my precautions against el Hiena's surprising us annoys you." He took a step forward, his curly hair tossed by the strong wind which at night swept that region. "Do you know, it's really amazing how clever that guerrilla is? A real mind reader he seems to be. So far," he emphasized the words, "he seems to have been able to foresee everything I intended to do.—It astonishes you, doesn't it, my dear captain?"

"*Madre de Dios!*" snarled Ribera. "You shall answer for this foolishness!—You will learn what it means to insult a loyal Mexican gentleman."

"Indeed?" As he spoke, Mike's hand was tapping lightly the holster of that heavy Colt which in other days had hung at the belt of his father, Colonel Lockheed, and in the moonlight his blue eyes were terrible as he said, "Loyal, eh? Then surely you won't object to my searching you?"

"No!—You shall die for this."

Clawing at his holstered pistol, Captain Ribera sprang back. But unfortunately for him, it was to land in the sinewy arms of ex-Sergeant Spurr.

"Steady, you damned grease ball, or I'll break your dirty neck!"

"Search him," directed Mike. "Guards, arrest this man!"

While the rest of the Mexican officers looked on in mingled horror and dismay, the rangy Texan fumbled beneath the dragoon's yellow uniform, presently to produce from its coat lining a few sheets of paper which bore the indubitable evidence which warranted the prompt hanging that ensued.

BUT ALL WAS not easy in Mike's mind when that grotesque black figure dangling from the ceiba tree at last swung quiet. In the last moments before he was swung to Eternity, Ribera managed to push out the gag; and amid furious incriminations, he screamed:

"You to-day, but el Hiena to-morrow! El Hiena will avenge me, and you will die such a death as mothers will use for frightening their children!"

"Too bad," Mike said as he passed Escandón, the likeable young lieutenant of *caçadores* who commanded the infantry. "Don't take it too hard."

The Mexican was sitting with face buried in his hands, but he looked up when Mike halted.

"*Dios!*" he cried bitterly. "Another traitor. No wonder the Gringos despise us! What curse is there on my people that so few of them can be true to their country? Oh, *coman-*

dante," he held out an imploring hand, "I pray you to please believe that we are not all like this swine! Hundreds of us would die a dozen deaths for the cause of our country's liberty."

"Never mind, *amigo*," Mike said gravely, "there are traitors in every army. I am trusting you as I would my father."

Already the eastern mountains were showing up with greater clarity, and as he stalked through the encampment, Mike realized that it was only a question of a short hour before he and Andrew would hurl themselves at each other's throats in a grim struggle that must end in death for one or for the other, unless—?

5

AT THE ROAD

A WOOLLY, GRAY-WHITE mist was still rising from that miniature grand cañon, through which flowed the Rio San Gorgio, while Comandante Lockheed strode back and forth. He was all-seeing and all-anticipating, as he marshalled his forces. Still enclosed in that ring of silent Yaquis, the Republican force left their horses behind and moved off to the rocky heights behind the ford. There, by the fading moonlight, they deployed, some taking cover in the dry part of the river bed itself, and others sheltering themselves behind tangled heaps of stone. The main body, however, Mike concealed along the crest of that bluff which commanded not only the ford, but the trail leading upwards to Las Estrellas, some three kilometers distant.

It was with a skill and sureness which commanded the esteem of that hardy veteran ex-Sergeant Spurr, that Mike threw out an extended line of skirmishers to the rear, and well out on either flank. For that last warning of the traitorous dragoon constantly rankled in his mind. He could visualize clearly that straggler whom he and Spurr had permitted to escape, as the fellow galloped off to tell el Hiena that both French and Republicans had retreated, leaving the immensely rich rancho of Las Estrellas quite defenseless.

That el Hiena would soon come riding onto the scene with his fourteen hundred cutthroats, Mike fondly hoped. What troubled him was just when and from what direction the wily guerrilla would appear. It ought to be soon, for the blood-thirsty rascal was very fond of dawn attacks; in fact, was celebrated for them.

His plan was a good one, Mike realized, yet the very cleverness of his maneuver was its greatest weakness. Let one single element fall short of perfect achievement and his intricate calculations—well, at least he would be no worse off than he had been before making this desperate attempt to wring victory from seemingly inevitable defeat.

Hatless, pistol in hand, he ranged back and forth above the ford, personally superintending the disposal of the bare-footed little *soldados.* And when the plovers commenced to whistle in the fields and the quail began to call their cheery notes, there was nothing to indicate that in the vicinity of the ford some four hundred very apprehensive men were tightly clutching their dew-covered rifles and waiting for the last dawn that many of them would ever see.

PANTING, DRIPPING WITH sweat, Mike at last flung himself down on the dewy grass between Lieutenant Escandón and Captain Zapatos. To them he said:

"You understand your missions clearly, gentlemen? When White, my bugler here," he indicated another one of those men from the ranch who formed his personal bodyguard, "blows a single note, your men are to prepare to fire. When he blows a second time, they are to fire and to keep on until he sounds 'cease firing.'"

"*Sí, señor comandante.*" Escandón's teeth glimmered in the fading darkness. "I am hoping that—"

"Quiet!" There was a little quiver in Mike's voice, for to his ear had come from far across the river a muffled, indistinct tramping. Was it cattle, coming down to drink?—No, a horse whickered softly, and Mike's heart surged. Undoubtedly, an armed force was advancing upon the ford.

The presence of the other force was further betrayed by the increased number of birds which, obviously alarmed, circled through the gray skies overhead, uttering frightened cries. Soon the dull, indistinct sounds commenced to become distinguishable. A horse snuffled, a bit jangled; somewhere a man tripped, fell and cursed when his rifle clattered among the stones on the invisible further shore. Otherwise, the stillness of impending doom ruled over the ford.

Mike realized that sweat was standing out on the backs of his hands; he could feel it prickle. Andy, too, was a great believer in early attacks. Were his brother's blue-clad legionnaires creeping down to the ford, along with their mounted Mexican allies?

He strained his eyes at the writhing, fleecy mist which clung tenaciously to the swift dark water of the river, as though loath to move away. A guarded voice was heard, but in what language it spoke Mike could in no wise tell, from his vantage point among the water smoothed bowlders.

He glanced sidewise, to glimpse the dark-faced Republican riflemen craning their necks where they crouched behind stones. They were pulling cartridges from their boxes and laying them conveniently to hand on the earth. Spurr, busy on his inevitable cud of "chawing," lay comfortably sprawled out on a flat rock fiddling with the sights of the Winchester which in his hands was as deadly as the thunderbolts of an Olympian god. Young Escandón, too, was feeling the strain. His lips kept moving, and he raised a dark green cuff to wipe away the sweat which had gathered on his well-shaped forehead.

Soon the noises grew very loud. Pebbles clicked against each other, and all at once Mike made out an indistinct black mass of mingled horsemen and infantry, pouring down over the other bank. One after another, the horses stiffened their front legs, and slid down to that sandy beach in a cloud of dust and gravel, their riders leaning back in their saddles and balancing themselves with their carbines. IT WAS STILL too dark to distinguish details when, with a queer buzzing evident in his finger tips, Mike saw the first of the enemy take to the water.

"How far across shall I let them get before I fire?" he asked himself.

"Get as many of them in the water as you can," a small inner voice prompted him.

Mike turned his head to find White already warming the mouthpiece of his trumpet in his mouth. The wide, white beach opposite was now alive with shapeless black figures. Like a sable flood they flowed to the edge of the ford, and now the splashing of water grew very loud. The leading horses seemed magically to grow shorter as the riders lifted their legs clear of the glassy black current. Ankle deep, knee deep, the leaders were across the deepest part now, and began to move out on that wet sand below.

As though mesmerized, Mike watched the progress of the first horseman towards the shore. He would count

*Could that be
Carolina, bound
and captive?*

three and then signal White to sound off. He was shaking,
he realized.—Good God, could Andy have walked into
this trap? What a perfectly fiendish turn of Fate, that he
should have to use his cunning against his own flesh and
blood. He would count three—and then order the bugle.

"One, two—" He never counted three, for the unexpected happened and a volley of shots rent the morning
stillness into a million deafening echoes. On the heights
across the river, beyond the horsemen fording the stream,
Mike could glimpse the golden-red flash of musketry.
Pandemonium broke loose in the ford as the wading horsemen reined in suddenly and huddled together.

"*Qué hay?*" Shrill voices called. "*Dios! Qué hay?*"

Clearly, this attack on the rear was a painful surprise to
the men below; but Mike, when he heard that shout in
Spanish, heaved a long sigh of relief.—El Hiena it was
who had fallen into his trap.

"Sound off!" he yelled, and the man called White set

the bugle to his lips. *Cra-a-a-a!* A single harsh note went pealing down the ford.

Like the sweetest symphony, there came to Mike's ears the sound of gun locks being cocked. *Cra-a-a-a!* The bugle brayed again, and suddenly the heights above the ford and the bluffs downstream became illuminated with brief, diamond-like flashes of fire. The Republican force was pouring a withering volley into the dismayed guerrillas, now half in and half out of the San Gorgio.

Louder swelled the uproar. The keening scream of bullets, the thwack of lead going home, the shrieks of wounded horses and stricken men rose from the ford.

WITH AN ALMOST theatrical effect the sun appeared suddenly above the distant Santa Lucrecia mountains, to cast an appropriately red glare upon the scene. A wild shout of surprise arose from the Republicans, for below there were no men in blue, no broad-shouldered Legionnaires, no green-clad Imperialists. Instead, there was a confused mass of furious, gaudily dressed bandits—el Hiena's creatures.

"*Viva la República!*" Mike's men yelled, and uttered exultant shouts as they perceived the perfection of their commander's generalship.

"*Carramba!* El Hiena is caught at last!"

"*Mira!* The French are behind them—"

Finding themselves unexpectedly on the rear of the bandit force, the Legionnaires forming up in steady ranks must have decided that one foe was as good as another. They were now pouring withering volleys into the disorganized bandit force.

"Hell, sir!" yelled Spurr. "This is neat! Them Frenchies are fightin' our scrap over yonder. And they got a heap more bullets than we have!"

Quickly, the battle lost shape. Cutthroats and murderers el Hiena's followers might be, yet they were good shots, and brave with that desperation of the cornered outlaw. Then, too, there were over a thousand of them, a force well outnumbering the combined French expedition and the Republicans.

In desperation, a party of mounted guerrillas, perhaps three hundred strong, spurred their mustangs and attempted to ride out of the trap and up to the heights on which the Republicans were posted. However, to do that they had no choice but to risk a gallop across almost the entire Republican front. Their effort was doomed before it began, and Mike was grimly pleased that not more than twenty-five or thirty wild-eyed guerrillas actually won free to run for dear life over the plains above. The rest of them lay in a weltering mass of dying men and kicking horses.

IN THE NEXT phase of the now desperate guerrillas' struggle to escape, most of their dismounted force joined in the general assault on the Republican position. Yelling and shrieking like fiends from the pit, they splashed across the ford and charged up from the water, dripping and scrambling hastily over the rocks. From behind them sounded the deep shouting of the French. *"Vive l'Empereur!"*

Then it was that Escandón's *caçadores* fired and reloaded as fast as they could, all the while yelling *"Viva la República!"*

Mike, engaged in emptying his revolver at the foremost bandits, now heard the rattle of ramrods off to the right and the distinctive banging of pistol shots increasing when the forces came to close quarters.

The gaudy ruffians hurled themselves up the yellow-red slopes, wildcats utterly regardless of losses.

But like sweet music to Mike's ears came the sound of the steady French volleys cutting down el Hiena's force from behind. The shallow water was choked with bodies now.

The scene at the ford became kaleidoscopic. Horses reared and plunged in water which was now tinged with red. Spray was flung high over the heads of the dismounted bandits. El Hiena would shortly learn that the heights were too well defended to be forced, and so would recoil to fight his way out through the French position.

A man on a magnificent buckskin stallion seemed to be directing the efforts of the guerrillas, and Mike was just pointing him out to Spurr when a throng of the desperate outlaws came charging up among the rocks.

Mike whipped up his revolver and sent a bullet smacking between the staring eyes of a rogue who wore a necklace of gold pieces above a greasy shirt that had once been of red velvet. Another face sprang into the gap, and as Mike fired at it he heard bullets pattering against the stones all about.

Up, up surged the bandit attack, and now Escandón's riflemen began to give back, tangling with their own long sword bayonets as they went. A critical moment and no mistake. It was then that the firing of the twenty Americans from Las Estrellas turned the tide. Kneeling, the veterans of the Second Dragoons coolly sniped bandit leaders out of their saddles, to drop them kicking onto the blood-splashed stones. Calmly, they crammed fresh cartridges into their Winchester breeches as though for all the world they were shooting turkeys at a fair.

"To the rear! To the rear!" He on the buckskin stallion was raging back and forth, shouting and waving.

"Must be el Hiena himself," bawled Spurr. "Ten bucks ye miss, Hank!—I'm outta shot, damn the luck!"

Mike had a good look at the famous guerrilla. An indescribably evil countenance was that of the silver-trimmed rider. He had a vulture's beak of a nose, dominated by a cruel slash of a mouth and small, close-set eyes.

AS A WAVE retreats down a beach, so the guerrillas, now reduced to six hundred desperate rascals, retreated across the ford, all the while harassed by the fire of the Republican forces, which had promptly returned to their positions.

"And now them Frenchies will have their crack at the bandits," panted Spurr. "There'll be a lot o' them fancy blue infantry bumped off afore long, 'cause they've drawn a line across the approach to the ford, and that line is too damn' thin to stop mounted men."

During the next ten minutes, Mike had the great pleasure of watching the French and the guerrillas become locked in a deadly struggle on the far bank. As he had astutely planned, every shot that was now fired made his own poignant problem that much easier. But, tempering this pleasure, was the realization that Andy was certain to be in the thick of the fight.

A further cause for reflection came home when he turned to Lieutenant Escandón who, smoke-blackened and dishevelled, came running up.

"Good God, sir," Mike roared. "Why have your men

stopped shooting? They can still polish off a lot of those guerrillas. They're still in easy range."

"If the *comandante* will find them ammunition," replied Escandón with a bitter smile, "they will continue to shoot. Almost the last cartridge has been spent. God help us if they or the French try to cross now.—We have only our bayonets."

"*Que lástima!*" groaned Zapatos as he ran up. "We must retreat at once."

"We stay where we are!" rasped the bareheaded young *comandante* in red.

"But what can we do when the French take their turn at the ford?"

"Well," replied Mike with a long sigh, "I've been figuring about that."

6

ALLIES FOR A DAY

DURING THAT INTERVAL in which the now wholly desperate guerrillas again formed in dense masses, this time to hurl themselves on the French ranks, Mike found respite for some rapid thinking. Up to the present, all seemed to have gone far better than he had dared hope. El Hiena, informed by the traitorous Ribera's messenger of the false retreats of both forces, had been lured into a dawn attack in which he had blundered into the French on their way to the ford. Not that it really mattered which enemy had got there first. Mike's strategy had simply been to catch one of his enemies between his own forces and those of the other enemy, so that perforce one side must be his ally in this tri-cornered fight.

Yet for some indefinable reason he felt uneasy. True, those guerrilla forces milling on the other shore were very numerous, but were there all of fourteen hundred men? Hardly. Where, then, were the rest of them? Perhaps they had gone on to that retreat which el Hiena maintained in the hills to the southwest. Perhaps they had seen the trap and had fled from it.

Deep in thought, Mike saw the guerrillas charge upwards, then glimpsed the long French bayonets flash and dip amid the vari-colored detachments of bandits. How el Hiena's men fought! Their broad-bladed machetes were doing a lot of execution among those steady ranks in blue and red.

"Hold 'em, Andy!" he yelled, though his voice was quite lost in the inferno of sound rising from the ford. Mike saw that sheer weight of numbers was forcing the French line to fall back.

"Damn it all," snarled Spurr, "he'll bust through!"

"*Dios!*" panted Captain Zapatos, his thin features working. "See, el Hiena will get away!"

Presently, el Hiena did break through, decimated and badly mauled to be sure, but none the less free to reorganize his savage horde and continue his indiscriminate war against civilization.

Moodily, Mike watched Escandón's infantry jump out from their hiding places and, like so many green-clad apes, go swarming down to the litter of bodies on the beach and in the water. There they snatched cartridge belts and rifles from the fallen raiders. Now and then a guerrilla, shamming death, would be discovered, and there would ensue a brief struggle, after which the *caçador* would go on, leaving yet another bandit to drain his life's blood into the reddened San Gorgio.

"Oh, God! If only we had ten rounds per man!" Bitterly Mike cursed the lack of ammunition. "We could smash both of 'em now."

His expert eye saw such a golden opportunity as soldiers pray for. What a chance to marshal his men now, to fling them across the ford and so fall tooth and nail upon the French before the Legionnaires had time to re-form from their encounter with el Hiena. Lacking ammunition it was suicide.

Furthermore, he was still troubled by those sharp misgivings concerning the whereabouts of the missing part of el Hiena's force. *Where in hell were they?* There must undoubtedly have been some real meaning to the taunt of the traitor Ribera.

"*Carramba!*" Zapatos cried, pointing wildly. "See, el Hiena breaks through! The French fall back—"

"Yeh," commented Spurr, "but in good order. Them's *muy soldado* fighters, in blue."

THERE WAS NOT so much shooting now. Mike peered through the swirling dust clouds and saw knots of dismounted bandits and Legionnaires fighting hand to hand, oblivious of a brisk cavalry encounter which was taking place off to the right. Suddenly the guerrilla cavalry slashed a path through the Imperial Mexican Lancers and galloped off to the south in a frantic, headlong retreat that was quickened by the spears of the lancers.

"Lord, look at 'em go!" yelled Spurr over the tumult. "The ornery scum! They're leaving their infantry behind."

And so it was. With that overwhelming selfishness of men who fight only for themselves, the mounted guerrillas raced off, pursued by the furious curses of their doomed and deserted mates.

"Nice, neat job," commented Mike when he saw the thoroughness with which Andy threw in a platoon of lancers on the bandit infantry's flank. In a twinkling those lancers in red and green had ridden over the guerrillas as a wave rolls over a beach. Then the Legionnaires charged with a deep, heart-stirring shout; their red pantaloons shining brightly in the light of the newly risen sun.

Thus the first phase of the struggle for the fords of San Gorgio came to an end.

"And now, gentlemen," quoth Mike, his young face very serious as he donned his tall shako and secured the strap under his chin, "I want a flag of truce.—Our only chance is to stop fighting and talk a little."

He had just turned aside from instructing Captain Zapatos to raise a white flag on a lance, when up from the rear pounded a galloper on a lathered horse. Disaster was written all over him, from his wounded head to the trembling legs of his mount.

"*Comandante!*" he stuttered, raising a blood-spattered hand in salute. "*Dios!* What a tragedy!"

While an icy flood seemed to pour into Mike's chest, he turned in his saddle. "Speak up, *tonto!* What has happened?"

"Las Estrellas—*Que lástima!* May the good Virgin protect us! That *teniente* of el Hiena called Sanchez the Black, crossed by—ford of—Angeles, above, while you fought here.—He fell upon Las Estrellas and—and—*por Dios, comandante,* I cannot tell—more."

SAVAGELY KICKING HIS horse forward, Mike covered the distance between himself and the half-incoherent galloper and seized the wild-eyed dragoon by the shoulder.

"Answer me, miserable one! What else has happened?"

The dragoon peered up through the tangle of blue-black hair that had fallen over his brown forehead. "I—I—*Aye de mi, no es—!*"

"Speak!"

"*El coronel,* your father—may the angels take mercy on his soul—"

"What happened?" cried Mike in a terrible voice. "Answer me, *hombre!*"

"They—The guerrillas murdered him, *señor comandante.* They shot him in his bed, after he had killed three of them—"

Mike took the blow as an officer and a gentleman should. His eyes closed briefly, and his big hands tightened on his tarnished silver belt until the material buckled.

"You—are sure—*el coronel*—is dead?" How pale the sunlight seemed! His father, Colonel Frederick Lockheed, dead!

"*Sí, señor comandante.*"

Then, over the initial anguish, came a second thought, a fear that he hardly dared voice. Mike's blue eyes were bright with anxiety as he said, "And—what of the Señorita de Luria?"

Before the regard of that tall figure in red, the dusty messenger dropped his eyes.

"She—she is gone, *señor comamdante.* The men of Sanchez dragged her away. From my hiding place in the mesquite I saw her led away on a horse as the column galloped away."

Carolina! Dainty, lovely Carolina! In the hands of el Hiena, and in his hands at a time when that human tiger would be raw with wounds and more than commonly ferocious because of the losses he had suffered.

"Which way did they go?" Mike demanded as he gathered his reins with the fumbling motions of a sleepwalker.

"Back towards the Ford of the Angels, *señor comandante.*"

"Thank you."

Then, as though the matter were entirely dismissed from his mind, Mike drew himself up and trotted back to the group of anxious faced officers who stood waiting beneath the flag of truce.

"Forward!" he cried, signalling ahead the gorgeous lancer from whose lance point a handkerchief snapped in the breeze.

SOME TEN MINUTES later the brothers met again in the center of the ford, under the eyes of their men. Andy, hollow-eyed and determined, was astride a powerful but ugly black charger, and Mike was riding el Aquila, that golden bay which was the pride of his heart. Watchful, suspicious and anxious, the two armies stood looking on from the heights at either side—those who were not occupied in ministering to the wounded or collecting the dead.

"Neat work, Mike," said Andy as his hand flickered to his scarlet topped *képi*. "Dad will be pleased with you.—I don't know how you maneuvered el Hiena between you and me but—well, you sure made me do a lot of your work. I didn't mind, however. As I may have told you, General Lorençez has a lot of scores to settle with el Hiena. In fact, I have definite orders to exterminate him."

As he saw the stricken expression in his brother's eyes he spurred forward, hand extended. "Hey, Mike—what's wrong, boy? You look terrible. You—you're not wounded?"

Then Mike told him the whole bitter truth, whereat the soldier in blue bent his head over his saddle, crushed with the double sorrow.

"Poor old Dad!—I—I wish—Oh, hell, it's the way he wanted to go, Mike—facing the enemy. I'll bet he took some of 'em with him—he always kept a pistol under his pillow.—But Carolina!" A stricken look came into his clear gray eyes. "Mike, Mike! In God's name what are we going to do?"

"It's very simple," replied the officer in red, while el Aquila thrust his sleek muzzle into the current lapping about his legs. "You say you have orders to exterminate el Hiena? Well, so have I. We also have orders to fight each other. But my orders don't say which must be done first—"

"Nor mine either!" Andy's long body stiffened and his unshaven jaw tightened. "By heaven, that's the ticket! We'll agree to an armistice. My men have had a heavy morning. I've between fifty and sixty casualties; and they couldn't attack you in your present position with much success."

"No, you couldn't," Mike hastily assured the French commander, and cursed himself for a liar when he thought of the empty cartridge boxes of his men.

"Well then, we're temporary allies."

"Yes. Allies until el Hiena is hanged and Carolina either rescued or—Oh, God, Andy, we've got to save her! You don't know what he does to women—pretty women."

A few moments more the two commanders arranged the details of their strange alliance, then each wheeled his horse and, sad faced, splashed back to his command. No doubt, Generals Lorençez and Juarez would have been deeply puzzled to hear their troops loudly cheering those very men whom they had been sent to fight.

7

"DESERTERS"

"GOOD LORD! THAT'S a regular fortress the old buzzard hangs out in," gloomily observed Andrew Lockheed, captain of the Seventh Company, First Regiment of the Imperial Foreign Legion. He lowered the field glasses through which he had been studying the distant loom of a yellow-gray ruin known to date from Aztec days.

"That's el Hiena's den, all right," replied Mike Lockheed, moodily stepping back from the leafy screen behind which the reconnaissance was taking place. "A mean place to tackle, too. I don't like the looks of those open stretches leading up to the walls. I suppose you know it'll cost a heap of men to storm that ruin."

The officer in blue pulled the cracked patent leather of his *képi* visor lower over his eyes, to shade them from the glare of the afternoon sun that was strongly reflected from the yellow soil of the uplands.

"Looks like pretty rough ground leading up to it," he commented hopefully. "We'd have cover most of the way, but that last three hundred yards to the walls is what'll do the damage."

In silence both officers studied the distant ruin, an oblong high walled edifice with crumbling towers rising at varying intervals. Then Mike turned in his saddle to view the long column which all day long had plodded silently onwards amid a drifting haze of dust.

In the depths of that broad *arroyo* they had followed for over an hour the expedition had halted in column. At the head of it had marched Andy's two hundred-odd veterans of the Foreign Legion, their hairy chests bared and their muskets canted every which way. Yet their hobnailed shoes had eaten up the distance faster than the ponies of the lancers which until recently had been commanded by the late Captain Ribera. Big, bearded, and talking in languages half of which Mike could not recognize, the red-pantalooned Legionnaires had swung tirelessly along, bent under their tall packs and cursing the dust.

After them had marched the pick of Lieutenant Escandón's *caçadores,* regulars of the Mexican line; but they looked very small and narrow-shouldered alongside the big Europeans. Following these came the mounted Yaquis, dark, narrow-faced, and splendidly muscled. In a loose column they rode in their customary silence, red loin cloths and brow bands weaving a perpetual design of color. Last of all were posted some fifty of Andy's green-and-red-uniformed Imperial Lancers, grumbling at the dust in which they must ride perforce. Quite a martial array it was, totalling four hundred of the best of both armies.

But when Mike raised a short telescope and once more studied those curiously carved but still stout battlements, his heart sank. He was fully aware that in arranging this expedition he was stretching Provisional President Juarez's orders to the full limit of their interpretation. Very well he knew that that doughty Indian patriot would not forgive the loss of too many men. Equally well, Mike realized that an open assault on the ruined fortress would pile up a casualty list which would gray the hair of any commanding officer.

"Yes, it's goin' to be a tough job." Andy observed as he put away his glasses. "If we only had a few pieces of artillery, we could knock that interestin' relic into brickbats. I asked for some, but General Méjia is so all-fired scared of an attack on his flank that he—"

THE LEGION OFFICER fell abruptly silent, as though aware he had been indiscreet, and his gray eyes flickered sidewise. But Mike seemed entirely absorbed in studying the approaches of that ancient Aztec fort.

Lieutenant La Marche wiped his sunburnt forehead and fanned himself with his *képi*.

"How far away is it?" he inquired. "It seems as though one could reach out and touch it."

"A good twelve kilometers," Mike replied. "It's the clear air up here, you know, that makes it seem so close. We won't get near it until sundown. You forget that my infantry have no boots or shoes."

"Marvelous!" declared La Marche, blinking behind his eyeglasses. "I marvel at these little Mexicans, so thin, so small, yet so enduring. Truly, they would become a great race had they leaders worthy of them."

"They have one, sir, in President-General Benito Juarez," Mike assured him warmly. "According to his lights, General Juarez is as determined, as brave and as honest as was our George Washington in the States. You've got a real man fighting against your emperor!"

"Well, gentlemen," began the senior Foreign Legion

officer, his glance taking in the dust-coated faces about him from which eyes peered as from behind grimy masks. "It seems to me that the time has come for a pow-wow. Unless the guerrillas in the ruin yonder have the eyes of hawks, they won't have seen us as yet."

"Does *el señor capitan* forget about the dust clouds we have raised?" suggested Escandón politely, as he pulled a handkerchief from his tunic bosom and wiped away some of the dust from eyes that had become red-rimmed through irritation.

"There's a lot of loose cattle and mustang herds hereabouts," came Mike's assurance. "So long as they see nothing more than dust they're not like to become suspicious."

"An attack in force," suggested Lieutenant La Marche, resettling the glasses on his narrow, aristocratic nose, "is the best solution. Those walls are low and not as strong as they seem. Our Legionnaires, with their bayonet points, will have small trouble in cleaning out yonder nest of rats."

"And I, I have my *caçadores,*" broke in Lieutenant Escandón eagerly. "They have a score to settle with el Hiena. Several of our men deserted to him, so we are particularly anxious to take them prisoner. Before the whole Republican army, we are going to execute them as a warning."

"Indeed?" said La Marche over his shoulder. "El Hiena is impartial. Two Irish rascals of my platoon deserted to him last week, and many of Méjia's men went with them."

WHILE THE WEARY troops squatted on the hot, dusty earth and took brief pulls at their gourds and felt-covered water bottles, Mike sank to his heels, balancing there like a huge red frog. One by one, the other officers also seated themselves on the warm earth, the bright sunshine striking through the leaves overhead giving them a queer mottled look.

"Think you could do it, Andy?" inquired Mike. How familiar that handsome, quiet brother of his looked as with brows knitted, he plucked and fell to chewing a blade of sweet grass.

"Sure, the Legion could do it," came the Legionnaire officer's reply, "but the general would raise hell if we got a flock of casualties. I'm not such a fool as to think we'd not lose every other man in a frontal attack on a position like that."

Mike inclined his blond-red head in assent. "Right, *hermano mío.* El Hiena's probably got fifteen hundred cutthroats living in that ruin up there. Along with—" he hesitated. Besides them, he had the beautiful and gracious daughter of the de Lurias. Sickened, Mike recalled details of certain skillful and subtle outrages practiced on women captives by this renegade from civilization. What was it? Oh yes—the luckless captives were forced to perform lascivious, vile dances such as the *hodiadah,* the *cumdavle* and the Yucatan tango. God help the poor, tearful creatures who, half clothed or wholly naked, must pirouette and caper before the vulgar and debased rabble which followed that shrewd and soulless bandit called el Hiena— the Hyena! Imagine Carolina—

Abruptly, Mike returned to the subject in hand, conscious that Andy, too, had been following something of the same train of thought.

"No!" Mike said suddenly. "A frontal attack won't do."

"No? Then please, what is to be done, *monsieur le commandant?*" demanded Lieutenant La Marche, with a touch of asperity. "We have no artillery, no sappers and no supplies to undertake proper siege operations. Bah!" he said. "Why waste time? Let us carry the ruin with the bayonet."

"All I can suggest is a night attack," said Andy somberly. "It'll cut down losses, but it'll also throw away the advantage of our better shooting. In the dark it's damned hard to do any effective shooting."

For several moments the four officers squatted in dismal silence, the two in blue, the one in red, and the one in green. They were alike only in their deep perplexity.

AT LAST MIKE raised his sunburned head, threw away the twig with which he had been drawing aimless designs in the dust and said, "Well, gentlemen, it seems to me there's just one way out of this. I'll grant it's a risky proposition, but here it is."

Three pairs of eyes sought his, Escandón glancing up from the cigarette he was rolling, Andy from the stained and greasy map he had spread before him and La Marche, the aristocrat, almost contemptuously.

"You say you've lost some men through desertion to el Hiena?" Mike said to his brother.

"Yes. In every outfit there are a certain number of bums who break away at the first chance they get. When we set sail from Oran we had a lot of recruits; they had filled the battalions in a hurry. Some of the new men weren't much good."

"Um!" grunted Mike. "So much the better."

"So much the better?" Surprise was in the voice of all three listeners.

"Yes. Here's what I propose. Suppose we fix up a bunch

of men—hand picked of course—and make 'em look like deserters. We'll go up to the ruin and try to argue those *mal hombres* to lettin' us inside the walls. I don't think el Hiena has ever seen me—"

"Hey! Hold on!" objected Andy, raising a sunburnt hand. "Do you really think you can get away with a thing like that?"

"Certainly, or I wouldn't have suggested it."

"No, no! It's not the idea I'm kicking about. It's your going into the fort. That's my job."

And Mike, with the image of pale, sad Carolina in his mind, shook his head until his yellow-red hair glistened in the hot sunlight.

"*De nada!* Remember, I outrank you, Bud. You are only a *capitaine,* and I"—with a mock heroic gesture he slapped himself on the chest, thereby raising a small cloud of dust—"am a major!"

"The Virgin protect us! What madness is this?" demanded Escandón, eyes very white in his dark, facile visage. "*Mira,* Don Mike, have you heard what this el Hiena does to spies? He strips them naked and flays them alive with bull whips, then uses their skins to cover his baggage boxes. A gentle man is this bandit! Should he feel merciful, he stakes his prisoner out and pours melted lead on his belly—"

"*Silencio!*" Mike cast his subordinate a withering glance. "I know all that. There are nevertheless many good reasons why such risks should be run. Now, gentlemen, listen to orders." He silenced the others with a sweeping motion of his hand. "I'll want ten Legionnaires, no more than that. The guerrillas would be suspicious of a larger number."

"You'll have them," promised Andy. "But you mustn't take such risks.—I'll go. Why should you risk your neck?"

Mike's steady blue eyes answered the question, then his laugh, infectious in its quality, rang out briefly.

"Oh, don't fool yourself that I'm hogging the fun. You'll have the main attack to run. You'll have to bring our men up there to the main gate under fire. When and *if* we get it open, you're the hero who'll have to lead a charge through it—"

So the four officers plotted, proceeding step by step over the plans and arrangements until they were satisfied that all that could be foreseen had been provided for.

SOME FIVE MINUTES after the conference was finished, Mike heaved his long figure to its feet and in a very aimless fashion strolled off towards the tired horses. But there was a lively gleam in his eye when, with a covert flick of his forefinger, he summoned Spurr, the long-limbed Texan whose cheek was, as usual, bulging with a quid.

"Sergeant," Mike murmured, under cover of adjusting a stirrup leather, "my brother let drop something awhile ago. He said that that old renegade *Méjia* was afraid of a cavalry attack on his flank—which, by the way, *is* wide open. You go"—he was very serious now—"and pick out a brace o' riders who have sense enough to stay off the skyline. Send 'em to me quickly, and I'll give 'em two all-fired important dispatches. One man is to ride hell-for-leather to General Juarez, the other to Frank Baldwin at Cattle Station Number One."

"Yes, sir," drawled the Texan, scratching his thin sandy colored hair. "But why that greaser general is scairt of cavalry attacks on his flank, is one on me. The whole dern countryside knows that all but a troop o' our cavalry are campaigning up Guadalajara way. 'Tain't nowise possible to—"

"Sergeant, you're going to have a flock of flies nesting in your mouth in a minute," snapped Mike. "Use your head about this. It may mean our necks! Now you *andar* along and get those riders ready. Give 'em the pick of the horses, and tell 'em if they let the guerrillas catch 'em I'll hang 'em again."

After delivering two brief but earnest dispatches to the narrow-eyed, tight-lipped range riders whom Spurr brought up, Mike turned back to the council. "The whole mess may never get to that stage," he reflected. "But as the old man used to say, 'One may just as well look at the third rise ahead, while he's studying the first.'"

IN THE CAREFUL preparations for the attempt to penetrate el Hiena's stronghold, Mike and Andy found some measure of refuge from the gnawing anxiety which was consuming them.

"Here are your men—all good scrappers," said the Legion officer. "This is Sergeant Dubonnet."

A grizzled giant with a long, purple scar disfiguring his right cheek from eye to chin point, saluted abruptly. He stood with the nine other Legionnaires, as bedraggled looking specimens of soldiers as one could hope to find anywhere outside of Turkey.

Dirty, artistically dishevelled, clad in parts of their own uniforms, from which some buttons and epaulets had been ripped and which were further equipped with a miscellany of garments from their Mexican allies, the Legionnaires seemed indeed an unholy collection.

The detachment, all blinking in the sunset, consisted of three Frenchmen, two Germans—Meier and Hoff by name—a villainous looking Spaniard called Perronegro, or Black Dog. Then there were two Greeks, bandy-legged but powerfully built fellows with glittering and restless black eyes, and—last but not least—three huge, blond Russians who seemed hopelessly stupid.

Presenting an odd contrast to the Legionnaires were a brace of nearly naked Yaqui Indians, puma-like in their graceful, powerful motions; two or three *caçadores*, and half a dozen dismounted troopers of the late Captain Ribera's *encurado* force.

Mingling with them, and not an obvious leader, was Major Mike Lockheed, completely disguised in a wine-spotted and ill-fitting green uniform of a corporal in the Fijo de Mexico battalion.

"I wish you wouldn't do this," Andy urged. "Let me take the chance. It's three to one that el Hiena'll smell a rat; so soon after a battle he's bound to be unusually suspicious. God knows what I'd do if he catches you. God! Every time I think of that hot lead and the bull whips—"

"He won't catch me, old boy!" replied Mike with assurance he was far from feeling. "Just you have that attack organized. When I blow this whistle, you'll know we've got the gate open and that it's all right to charge in. Wait until you hear that whistle, for I aim to start a ruckus in that kennel over yonder that'll give the guards something to think about besides what is goin' on outside the walls. *Entiende?*" Mike's engaging smile flashed in the semi-darkness. "Otherwise, you could never get across that quarter mile of bare ground."

"We'll be there," Andy promised grimly. "But if you weren't my commanding officer, I'm damned if I'd let you get away with this."

"Forget it, Bud," quoth Mike soberly. "It's you that Carolina loves—not me."

8

EL HIENA'S DEN

THE SUN, DROPPING into a raging sea of red clouds, touched with a brush of fire the brass work on the ill-adjusted and miscellaneous equipment of that little band of stragglers. Vigorously waving a none too clean white handkerchief, they came swaggering in loose disorder up the weed-grown path leading to the ancient Aztec citadel.

Mike noticed here and there beside the trail curiously carved stones, half hidden by myrtle and mesquite. Many times, when hunting for strayed cattle, had he viewed this ruin from a distance; but never had he appreciated what a really solid piece of masonry it still was.

By tilting back his tangled red head he could make out frowning, vine-grown walls sharply silhouetted against the red radiance of the evening sky. Yes, he could even distinguish the grotesque plumed serpent heads which, like gargoyles, jutted boldly out from wall angle and the top of the crumbling tower.

"*Oíga!* Up there on the wall!" he hailed. A row of sombrero-crowned heads appeared, peering over rifle barrels. A long instant they regarded with manifest suspicion the motley group below, and more especially that figure in the shabby corporal's uniform.

"*Qué hay?*" "Who are you?" "What do you want?"

"*Nom de Dieu!*" bellowed the huge Legion sergeant. "Who are we, *mes amis?* Why we're men grown sensible enough to quit fighting for a lot of gold-decked officers— eh, Jacques? Eh, Lucien? Yes, we're men who have learned that it's better to risk one's own carcass in one's own interest. Is it not so?" He turned to the Greeks, who shouted some assent in their own language.

"*Gewiss,*" yelled Hoff, waving a wine bottle. "Here's to freedom. *Hoch, hoch, die Freiheit!* Let us in. Good fighters we are—"

More shaggy, evil heads appeared along the weed-grown battlements above; and the murmur of voices grew louder when the stragglers, some twenty-two in number, halted before a modern gate which was constructed of very massive timbers and iron rivets.

"Open! Open!" yelled the dismounted *encurados* waving their *escopetas.* "Open, *hermanitas,* we are hungry. Old Juarez—may God blacken his face!—feeds us ill."

And so the motley throng below the gate clamored for admittance, the disordered Legion uniforms mingling with the more gaudy uniforms of the Republican army.

Then some one in authority appeared on the walls.

"Keep these rascals covered," directed the newcomer, a dark featured villain in an orange velvet coat that glittered with gold. "And you, Chico the Zambo, tell old Red Hands to open the gate."

"*Ça va,*" whispered one of the Frenchmen with a nervous grin, "those *vauriens* are going to let us in."

BUT THE EXPRESSIONS of the pseudo deserters were not what they should have been, Mike decided. By the fading light their eyes were too tense, too anxious, too apprehensive to be natural. Accordingly, he warned them in undertones.

"Play the game well, or it'll be short and painful."

On hinges that screamed like a man in agony, the ponderous gate was swung back, exposing more and more of a gaping black entrance in which nothing could be seen.

"Come in, you who would join us," directed the man above the gate, and Mike sensed that there was that in his voice which hinted at deadly possibilities.

Their weapons canted every which way, straggling like the masterless men they counterfeited, the twenty-two advanced boldly into the ominous inner gloom, but more than one sweating hand took a convulsive grip on knife hilt or pistol butt.

Mike, swaggering along with a brace of dragoon pistols tucked in a faded blue sash, could hear the wild hammering of his own heart above the dull reverberations of his footsteps, which were caught and flung back by the chill masonry all about.

Talking, gesticulating and bragging to lessen their fear of a sudden deadly volley, the impostors at last came out into the open air again and found before them a vast courtyard in which smoldered countless small fires. Women's shrill voices could now be distinguished above the yapping of hundreds of dogs and all the other noises associated with a camp. They felt better—*Dios*, there was a smell of smoke and cooking in the air!

The ruin, as Mike swiftly discovered, was infinitely more spacious than he had at first imagined. Fully fifteen hundred men, together with their women and their horses, were enclosed within the towering, plant- and vine-covered walls.

Typical of such encampments was the complete lack of order. Bedding, saddles, arms and loot of all kinds lay scattered about. Dozens of horses kicked and snapped on a single picket line that was fit for only twenty. Several hundred other raw-ribbed mounts were jammed indiscriminately into a ramshackle corral of wood that ran half the length of the far wall and gave off a choking stench of manure and ammonia. Mike could glimpse the scrawny mustangs stretching their thin necks to nibble at leaves on the vines above.

Squatting, standing and lying about the smoking little fires, were the vast majority of the bandit throng; and many of them, as the new arrivals noticed, with deep, if covert satisfaction, wore reddened bandages.

WHEN THE AMAZED newcomers, blinking in the smoke and stench, were well inside they were immediately set upon by the usual swarms of ravenous dogs, as much a part of Mexican life as *tortillas y frijoles.* However, a few well directed kicks and blows dispersed the mongrels, and then the interlopers found themselves free to study a semicircle of dark, menacing figures hemming them in. Armed to the teeth, this guard detachment held their guns at significantly ready positions.

"Halt where you are, and keep your filthy paws still," directed a heavyset individual who wore a dirty blue hussar jacket and the yellow pantaloons of an officer in the Imperial Queretaro Regiment. In his hand he carried a huge machete that gleamed red in the uncertain firelight. Half suspiciously, wholly contemptuously, he surveyed the intruders.

"Bah!" he sneered. "What a mangy pack of homeless curs.—*Por Dios!* José, did you ever see such disgusting swine?—Who are you, and what do you want?" he suddenly demanded of the newcomers.

Standing quite still, aware that death hovered very near at hand, the false deserters poured out a tale of grievous wrong, of scant rations, of scantier pay, of frightful punishments for slight infractions of discipline. A curious picture the pseudo-renegades made as they stood there, dwarfed by the great stone gate and hopelessly hemmed in by dense masses of scowling bandits.

"Is his honor, the illustrious protector of the poor who is called el Hiena here?" timidily demanded Mike, in the Jalisco accent.

"*Carrajo!* Stop sniveling and speak up. No, el Hiena is occupied. But he will be here at any moment. Lay down your arms."

"In for it, or I'm a blue shote," muttered Spurr. "Reckon our best bet is to obey orders and do what that grease ball says."

The Legionnaires, however, were loath to part with their familiar, true shooting muskets; and at their obvious reluctance an ominous growl arose from the dark-faced crowd which grew greater and more threatening moment by moment.

"Shoot them—"

"*Pronto!* Put down those arms or I'll have the filthy hide stripped off your shoulders," snapped the bandit leader, whose name appeared to be Fuertes. "Pile your weapons here in front of me. *Entrañas de Dios!* Be quick else I lose my patience."

Just then came a welcome diversion, for a black-haired rascal in the remains of a blue uniform came swaggering forward.

"Ah!" he jeered. "Sure and 'tis some o' the boys out o' that damned Legion.—So yez all finally got sense enough to quit?"

"Mais oui, here we are, *mon cher* O'Hara," replied Dubonnet as he tossed his musket onto the growing pile before the high-heeled boots of the fox faced bandit lieutenant.

"Glad to see yez here. I've a few scores to settle wid ye—" And the deserter stepped by, grinning evilly.

NO ONE SPOKE while Fuertes, still holding the carbine in his hand, studied face after face before him.

"You, the corporal," he said, pointing to Mike. "You are from where?"

"From Mascota, your honor," whined the impostor. "A very little town, your honor, but a good one."

"I think you lie," snapped the bandit lieutenant. "I seem to have seen you before somewhere. I never forget faces. Later I will remember and then—

"Now," he advised the disconsolate adventurers, "since we stand in need of recruits, I will let you live, on the chance that you may prove to be what you say you are. Meanwhile, you are prisoners until el Hiena decides your fate. You see, you mongrels, we take no chances."

The fellow's glittering eyes narrowed ominously as he jerked a greasy thumb to a narrow gate leading to a small courtyard opening off the main encampment.

"Get your filthy carcasses in there and meditate upon what can be done with hot lead. *Oíga*, you rascals!"

Turning, the amiable Señor Fuertes beckoned a gaudily clad lounger who stood with a cigarette dangling from the corner of his mouth. "Some beans and some water," he commanded.

"Beans! *Grand, nom d'un petit dieu bleu*," roared Dubonnet. "What welcome is this to new comrades?—Cold beans, cold water!"

As for the Yaquis, they snarled like teased wildcats and slunk off into the courtyard which had been indicated. Perronegro, the Spanish Legionnaire, bit his thumb at the mocking throng, then ripped out a string of blasphemous curses; and the *encurado* deserters taunted the guerrillas for their lack of hospitality.

"Silence!" roared Fuertes, waving his machete. "Another yelp out of you, you scum, and we will have some new saddle housings in the morning. No one asked you jackals to come here."

And so, within the brief space of five minutes, the now wholly dejected impostors found themselves under heavy guard, disconsolately drinking muddy tasting water and munching cold beans that were thickly coated with grease.

"*Du lieber Gott!*" growled Hoff, licking his stubby and none too clean fingers. "This is damn slim provender for the work we've got ahead."

"What work can we do—with no rifles, no knives?" grunted one of the Russians, who was gazing about at the fire-tinted walls with the sad uneasiness of a caged bear. "The doorway there is not very wide.—And now see what happens!" He pointed to a group of guerrillas who were

kindling a large fire, squarely in line with the battered
door to the courtyard. Beyond them stood perhaps thirty
or forty scowling bandits, each holding ready a carbine.
Decidedly, the amiable guerrilla lieutenant was taking no
chances.

What a fool he had been, bitterly reflected Mike, to
think, even to dream, that such an elementary plan as
this stood the faintest chance of success. He was grateful,
however, for the respite and the opportunity to study his
surroundings.

It was chiefly his inability to move about, to contrive in
some way that disturbance which he had planned in order
to shield the approach of Andy's force, that harassed him.
What could he and his men do, thus penned in the little
court and always under the eye of vigilant guards? Think
as he would, no feasible plan offered itself.

Already the stiff night wind which arose in that part of
the country with the setting of the sun was commencing
to stir the plants crowning the Aztec masonry.

DISSEMBLING HIS DESPAIR, Mike crouched cross-
legged on the cold, hard stones, just inside the portal.
Dubonnet and the rest of the Legionnaires, he realized,
were slouching sullenly around, watching what took place
down the courtyard. One of the *encurados* had produced a
flask of *pulque,* and the frowns of the Mexican members
of the imperilled detachment were lightening somewhat.

"Looks like they're fixing for a *fiesta,*" Mike muttered,
seeing certain guerrilla women tottering by, bent under
huge loads of wood. Others bore heavy earthen ollas that
gurgled pleasantly.

Before very long a huge fire was kindled and the brittle

tinkle of mandolins rose to drown the mournful call of the sentries posted on the wall. These, following the Mexican custom, hailed each other every five minutes with a long-drawn and almost musical *"Centinela alerta-a-a!"*

Bandits in soiled finery and their pretty, shrill-voiced drabs were gathering in a huge, tawdry, malodorous throng about the ollas, and soon gourd dipperfuls of *pulque* and *tequila* evoked raucous laughter, deep curses and the lilting measures of obscene song.

Silently, morosely, the man in the shabby corporal's uniform watched a dozen of the bandit leaders sprawl on a tall heap of hay, to lie there fondling their mistresses and beating their thighs in time to the strumming of the guitars.

But as Mike noted to his increasing distress, in spite of all the gayety below there was no relaxing of vigilance on the part of those guards on the walls and above the gate. Nor, for that matter, of those dark-faced cutthroats not thirty feet away. How in hell could he get out and create that disturbance which he must raise in order to give Andy his chance to dash across the bare spaces?

Suddenly Mike's perplexed musings were interrupted, he saw that everywhere bandits were scrambling to their feet and pulling off their weird miscellany of head pieces. Presently, from a door to the right of the great gate, there swaggered into sight a burly individual, picturesque as a painting by the old Spanish master, Goya. He wore a gaudy bolero of green velvet, the bosom of which was obscured by two crossed cartridge belts.

In this evil-featured man with the sweeping black mustachios Mike had no difficulty in recognizing the person who had ridden that buckskin stallion on the morning previous.

Dangling, gaudy rings of gold flashed in his ears, more golden flashes played in el Hiena's huge misshapen mouth, which Mike studied with interest not unmixed with disgust, for a nervous affliction made the guerrilla's lips writhe back continually from yellow, irregular teeth, as though he were convulsed with perpetual, hideous laughter. No wonder that they called this monster "el Hiena"!

MIKE'S HEART THUDDED a little more violently as he beheld, a few paces behind the dreaded guerrilla chieftain, two underlings, one of whom was leading a third figure in flowing white. The great bonfire suddenly flared skywards, casting a strong red light over the whole restless scene, and Mike's breath halted. Great God! Could that be Carolina who was tottering along at the end of a rope? Incredible! They would not dare to treat thus a daughter of the proud and powerful de Luria family.

But the fact remained. Sickened with horror, Mike, from among the shadows, watched the procession draw near.

He had reason to be proud of the girl whom he had loved and lost. None but Carolina could have kept her pride and her courage at such a moment. Even in her despair, her small, dark head was held high, and she seemed quite unaware that the lustrous torrent of her black hair flowed in loose disorder over shoulders which were more revealed than concealed by the single white shawl which was her only covering.

Two paces behind her reeled a huge, black fellow who grimaced and capered about like an evil child. He flourished a long-lashed bull whip, making it snap repeatedly in the air.

"Oh ho-ho!" he chortled, patting Carolina's quivering shoulder with a dirty paw. "You will dance, *por Dios* you will! A lovely dance, little silver feet. My *culebra* has a way of fitting wings to the feet of slow dancers."

Fury welled into Mike's breast when he saw tears glistening on Carolina's smooth cheeks. He beheld, secured to her slim ankles those golden bands which, trimmed with tiny bells, are an accessory to that undulating and suggestive gypsy dance called the *cumdavle*.

Mike alone could guess something of the agony that must be racking the soul of that pure and aristocratic young thing.

But she did not flinch, not even when the guerrillas about the fire began to yell insulting suggestions and invitations to her.

One gaunt rascal sprang atop the pile of fodder, a wild, fire-lit figure, and cupping his hands he shouted, "More wood on the fire, *amigos!* Much more wood. Let's not let our little dancer catch cold nor fail of enough light.— *Aprisa!*"

WHEN THE TRAGIC little procession was opposite the door in which Mike crouched, Fuertes, the lieutenant, called out something about the prisoners. El Hiena halted, glowered at the little courtyard, then spoke briefly with the leader of the guards. Mike saw the fellow's vulturelike head shake irritably three or four times, saw him cast a brief, lowering glance at the disconsolate men in the courtyard, his mouth twitching and jerking all the while.

"Deserters they said? *Carrajo! De ninguna mañera!*" Mike

Spurr clubbed his rifle.

heard him growl. "Deserters don't go off in big bands like that. Keep them under close guard. These Legionnaires are all devils.—When the dance is over we will attend to them in the customary manner."

So saying, el Hiena turned on the high heels of his boots. The enormous golden spurs that he wore flashed like twin beacons as he strode on towards the fire and the eagerly waiting multitude about it.

THE ONLY TOO well-founded suspicions of El Hiena made Mike sick at heart, and he was by no means encouraged when he saw that the guards became more watchful than ever. Mike slunk back to merge with the shadows; and in an undertone he repeated his alarming intelligence to the false deserters.

"Ay de mi! We are surely lost," groaned one of the Mexicans. "Let us break forth and die by the bullets of the guards rather than suffer—"

"We'll do nothing of the sort," snapped Mike, surveying the anxious, fire-lit faces of his followers. "The moon is nearly over the mountains now. Did one of you save a weapon out of the pile?"

Here and there hands were cautiously lifted, and a count revealed that three or four daggers and a brace of pistols had escaped the search of the guerrillas.

Like a furious tocsin there beat in Mike's brain a call to action. But how could he cause the very necessary and prolonged diversion? He *must* do something to prevent the shameful tragedy which would shortly be enacted before the roaring bonfire. God! Even now he could see the guerrillas lining up five deep, yelling, waving their ragged arms in anticipation.

El Hiena was talking to them, pointing to the pitiful little figure in white, and to one side the huge fellow with the whip was still swinging his strange weapon through the air with childish delight.

"I'VE BEEN HOPING," Mike stated to the malodorous men who were crowding about him, "that we could set fire to something. But now that's not possible. With those guards out there all set and waiting, damned few of us would live to get past that door; and some of us have *got to live long enough to get that gate open* for the rest of our men!"

Ex-Sergeant Spurr's leathery face loomed near, his deep-set eyes glittering in the light of those ever increasing flames.

"And what was it you was aimin' to set fire to?" he inquired hoarsely.

"Why, that hay and fodder pile over there." Mike pointed over the shoulder-high wall which fenced off the enclosure. "It's dry, and ought to burn like tinder."

"Um," grunted Spurr speculatively, "that shouldn't be so hard."

"*Nom de Dieu!*" Dubonnet, the big Legion sergeant made an unpleasant gesture. "Don't be an idiot. That pile is two hundred feet away. How many of us would live to get there—?"

"Wal," drawled the Texan, "just fancy that, Froggy. 'Tain't no wise necessary for any one to go yonder. I reckon there's a flint and steel among us, and maybe some tinder?"

He turned to Perronegro, the Spanish Legionnaire.

"*Oíga, Legionario,*" said he in flawless Spanish, "give me your knife."

"Why?" demanded the Spaniard suspiciously. "I can use it as well as you when the time comes."

Mike saw Spurr's slit of a mouth tighten, so he ordered the Spaniard, "Give it to him.—What's your idea, sergeant?"

Spurr balanced the stiletto speculatively before answering. "Wal, I'm pretty handy throwin' a knife, and if *I* ain't handy enough, I'll stake my life them Yaquis are. Now, sir, what I aim to do is to set some tinder afire, wrop it up in a handkercheef, and then tie said wipe to a dagger handle. I'll be a long, tall son of a buzzard if I can't stick this here knife into the fodder pile yonder. With this wind blowing—*entiende?*" He nodded significantly to a small banana palm which, sprouting from a ruined battlement, was swaying violently in the chill evening wind which springs up in Oaxaca.

In half a dozen languages the doomed adventurers uttered praises to God, and a few moments later flint was scraping steel until a large red coal glowed in a little heap of tinder carefully arranged on a silk handkerchief.

"Now two of you *hombres* start a row," snapped Spurr, as he rolled back his sleeve and again tested the weight of the knife between horny thumb and forefinger. "Ready, sir?"

"Hold on," said Mike. "We'd better wait a minute." It cost him much to say the next few words. "We'll—we'll have to wait until that dance begins, I guess. I don't want to risk anybody's seeing that knife fly through the air. Remember, this is our only chance."

SO, LIKE AMATEUR actors uneasily awaiting their cues, the doomed men squatted about their courtyard, conscious of the unblinking watchfulness of the guards beyond the gate, while Mike, grinding his teeth in impotent fury, watched what was taking place far down the main court.

"Gettin' set now," he murmured when, after a brief interval, several guitars accompanied by an accordion and castanets commenced to play that slow, sensuous measure to which the *cumdavle* is danced. Of its own accord, the excited crowd fell back, leaving a circle of bare stone some forty feet in diameter. On the far side of this cleared space the bonfire throbbed and flared, flinging up sparks which were twirled off to the westward by the rising wind.

As in the grip of an evil dream, Mike watched the giant with the whip step back and flourish the lash. The music swelled louder, more insistent. "*Vaya!*" yelled a thousand voices. But Carolina, now left quite alone, and hemmed in by a sea of faces, stood still, her supple figure outlined to the last detail by the fire light beating through the thin silken shawl. Suddenly the bandit's arm flashed back the whip licked out, and from the girl's lips burst a moan of pain.

Sweat sprang out on Mike's brow. God, how hard it was to stay where he was!

Again the lash cracked, and half involuntarily the girl dodged that burning lash. A great gust of laughter, fierce and evil as the cackle of so many jackals, broke out. While the wild music increased its tempo, the bull whip snapped; and again the figure in white reeled aside.

Mike glared about, saw that every face was now turned in the direction of the bonfire. All except the guards before the gate.

"All right," he said in a sibilant undertone. Promptly, two of the Legionnaires began a noisy dispute in which the others joined in.

It was on the far side of this milling tangle of prisoners that Mike stood, waiting the psychological moment. At his elbow was the Texan, wiry body poised and taut, a gleam in his eye, and the dagger in his right hand. From the small silken bag secured to the handle, smoke was now rising in a little curl.

"Reckon I'll have to throw right quick now," he warned. "The fire'll be burnin' the silk in a minute."

LICKING DRY LIPS, Mike studied the guards. Yes, all their attention was on the two cursing fighters who had now come to blows.

"Now!" he cried, and his heart seemed to surge up into his head as Spurr's long arm, swinging like the beam of a catapult, sent the dagger soaring high up into the sky—a glimmering ray of light.

Quivering in every nerve, Mike watched its trajectory, saw it flash briefly against the glowing stars, saw it reach the zenith of its flight and then plunge downwards with

a final shimmer of the blade before it vanished from sight
beyond the figures lolling on the forage pile.

"Overshot, damn it to hell!" grunted Spurr, pushing the
wind-whipped hair from his eyes. "Knew it the minute I
throwed."

"Maybe not," was Mike's tense reply. "Maybe it fell in
the loose hay on the far side." But he was far from sure.

"Better try another," the Texan urged.

"All right."

But unfortunately, during the pseudo fight the tinder
had been spilled to the ground, and there was no more.

Louder sounded the roars of the crowd. Mike resolutely
kept his eyes averted from that anguished silhouette whirling before the flames. It did no good now to watch the
tragedy being enacted down yonder.

He wondered where Andy was. Was he crouched with
his men at the top of that *arroyo*, waiting for the signal?

"Blast the luck! I must have thrown clear," Spurr snarled
and vented a string of sulphurous curses.

But just then the music faltered, voices rose in shrill
outcry, and horses began to trample and whinny with fear,
for from the back of the fodder pile a whitish column of
smoke was pouring. This, seized by the cold night wind,
was instantly whirled off into the darkness beyond the
vine-grown battlements.

9

BATTLE WITHIN WALLS

THE ENSUING FEW moments were for Major Mike Lockheed as agonizing and nerve racking as any he had experienced in all his brief but tempestuous career. He found himself wishing for a dozen eyes—one pair to watch the actions of those half-seen sentinels up on the ruined towers. Were they keeping their gaze fixed upon the broad mesa they were supposed to watch? Or were they watching the growing excitement below? Even more, Mike wished that he had a chance to see what had become of Carolina, poor fragile child! What she must be suffering! He could have used another pair of eyes to study the faces of his men. And last, but not least, it was vitally important that he watch the actions of the guards outside the gateway.

Doubts and questions flooded his brain. Just how much time should he allow Andy and his men to get across that three hundred yards of bare ground? Would he and his devoted twenty-one followers be able to stand off the bandits long enough to get the gate open and to keep it so? Could he find and protect Carolina de Luria from further harm?

"Nom de Dieu! Look! Look at the flames," cried Dubonnet, and his unshaven features were lit by a sudden glare as

a blinding sheet of flame sprang into being. Now the main
fodder pile had caught and the horses in the main corral
were backing in terror, screaming their fright.

All was confusion in the courtyard now. The revel-
ers, many of them thoroughly drunk, uttered shrill, high
pitched cries and ran aimlessly about. But by far the larger
part of the guerrillas obeyed the orders of el Hiena, who
raged back and forth, profanely ordering the wide-eyed
bandits to pull the fodder pile apart.

"I'll give Andy five minutes," Mike told Spurr. "That
ought to allow him time to distribute his men."

Clouds of smoke, spark-laden, came whirling down into
the courtyard where the prisoners crouched, and all of a
sudden flames burst out from a new point. Blazing straw
carried by the high wind had fallen on the thatched roofs
of certain *jacals* and set them afire. But under el Hiena's
directions, the guerrillas were slowly but surely checking
the flames.

A wild and desperate figure Mike made in his dusty
corporal's uniform, as he wheeled to face his followers.

"In a minute," he announced, wiping smoke induced
tears from his eyes, "I'll blow this whistle. When the
smoke's pretty thick, we'll all rush the guards. You Mexicans mingle with the crowd, spread fire—turn loose those
horses. *Entiende!*"

"*Sí, señor comandante!*" they cried. "*Viva la República!*"

"And what of us?" demanded one of the Russians, his
small blue eyes beginning to light as his Cossack blood
warmed to the prospect of fire and pillage.

"Legionnaires, follow me. Hold the gate—to the last
man. Each man must get a gun!"

From the throats of those bronzed veterans in dishevelled uniforms burst a low cry oddly at variance with the
first, *"Vive l'Empereur!"*

EVEN AT THIS harried moment, and even as he raised the
whistle to his mouth, Mike could not suppress a fleeting
grin. Not so bad to have Napoleon III's crack soldiers fighting his battle. True, he would have to fight them later, but
let the future wait!

Before he could blow the whistle, a shot, startling and
unexpected as a thunderclap on a clear afternoon, rang
out overhead. Mike shot an anxious glance upward, and
through the drifting smoke he distinguished a bareheaded
sentinel frantically waving his arms and pointing over the
wall.

"Alerta!" he screamed in the thin, womanish voice of the
average Mexican.

"Alerta!" Another sentinel was whipping up his rifle to
fire into the darkness beyond the wall.

Mike waited no longer. He blew one shrill note on his
whistle, then headed a wedge of men in a frantic sally
through the courtyard gate. Thank God, the smoke was
very thick! The guards were just waking up to the fact that
death was bearing down upon them.

In great leaps, Mike bounded across the twenty-odd feet
of clear space, felt his heart stop as a guerrilla in a brilliant
yellow shirt whipped up his *escopeta* and fired. Its bullet
whined past Mike's ear, and the other guards delivered a
wavering volley.

But there must have been something awesome about
those ten giants in disordered blue uniforms; and something particularly terrible about the gaunt Texan, Jake

Spurr, who, stirred to his depths, was shouting that fierce warcry of the old Southwest, "Goliad!—Remember Goliad!" Most of the bandit guards remained in paralyzed impotence.

Like a giant who has long been enslaved by pygmies, but who is free at last, the ex-sergeant of the United States Dragoons burst through the guard fire, whirling a clubbed rifle like a flail of death. Mike had glimpses of him, towering over the shorter Mexicans. And the Legionnaires, too, were fighting like devils.

Before the unexpected appearance and the desperate ferocity of their late prisoners, the guards fell back on the main body of the guerrillas. These, at el Hiena's orders, abandoned their fire fighting and now began to assemble in the center of the plaza. Most of them were for the moment without arms, and so a few precious instants were granted to the desperate twelve.

"Quick!" yelled Mike. He was conscious of the fact that from beyond the walls there now sounded a rousing shout, such as comes from the throats of four hundred excited men: "To the gate—to the gate!"

AS HE DASHED towards the gate, hurdling over the body of a bandit whose head had been caved in by the blow of one of the Russian Legionnaires, Mike felt his heart stand still. He had never realized that there were so many bandits inside this ruin. Great God! The far end of the courtyard swarmed with their tarnished finery. He could see dense hordes of them by the wavering fire light. Rapidly, they were taking positions.

"*Aprisa!*" yelled Perronegro, his eyeballs gleaming white

as he dashed the blood from a wound above his right eye. "They form for a charge!"

"Kick those saddles onto the ground," barked Mike, "make a breastwork! Some shoot while—rest—try to open—gate."

Sweating and panting, he steadied himself to fire at a couple of guerrillas who, pluckily enough, were attempting to defend the gate with their machetes.

Fire spurted from Mike's pistol, momentarily lighting up two sable faces contorted with excitement. Subconsciously he heard the distinctive *thock!* of his bullet going home. Powder fumes, hot and sour as the breath of hell, stung his nose, and he was dimly aware of a shadowy figure collapsing.

The guerrillas on the walls now were shooting as fast as they could. Louder swelled their yells and the crackle of musketry.

One—two, heavy wooden bars he heaved from their sockets, hurling them aside so that they fell with dull thumps on the stone paving beneath his feet.

Thwack, zwee-e-e! Plock! The guerrillas were pouring a deadly hail of bullets into that gloomy gate.

"Swing the gate!" Mike yelled. "Pull!"

A Legionnaire, tugging at Mike's side, uttered a shrill scream of agony and crumpled, momentarily blocking the gate. Frantic at the delay, Mike was forced to take time to haul the still shuddering body aside.

A great wave of sound came from behind. Risking a quick glance over his shoulder, Mike saw the entire guerrilla force bearing down on him and his handful, and with that frantic strength which is lent to the doomed, he heaved at the massive wooden door. Now it swung open, to reveal a steel-tipped column poised outside—wide eyes, *képis,* open yelling mouths....

"*En avant!*" The martial wave surged irresistibly forward, bayonets gleaming like surf, on over the bodies of those who had fallen while fighting to open the gate.

To avoid being trampled, Mike flattened against the stonework, watching the bearded veterans of Africa dash by on the double. Yelling like fiends they hurried past him, their sweaty faces red in the glare of the conflagration.

Promptly, el Hiena's men opened fire on the packed mass of Legionnaires filing through that gateway.

TWO WHOLE RANKS of Legionnaires who had just gained the courtyard fell as though cut down by the single sweep of a sickle. But a few managed to survive. These fell on one knee and began to fire steadily at that black mass of bandits who came sweeping onward to clear the gate.

Though the French, with indomitable courage, swept on through the entrance, the bullets of the bandits played havoc in their ranks. Hampered by the dead and dying, they began to fall into disorder.

All at once Mike knew that the French could not carry the passage unless something happened.

The night was now become a bedlam of sound and smell. Dominating everything was the deadly rattle of musketry which, in a measure, drowned out the shouts and shrieks of the fighters.

Forced flat to the entrance wall by the squirming mass of Legionnaires, Mike thought that the gateway to hell itself could not compare with such a scene; for the fire, now unchecked, roared ever higher, throwing the bandit force into sharp relief. Ammunition, perhaps that which had been captured the day before from Mike's own train, began to explode with deafening detonations.

All about him, men panted and swore, and the smell of hot wool and sweat was almost as strong as the sickish sweet reek of spilt blood and *torn* entrails.

"Fight, you devils! *En avant!* Keep moving!" There was Andy's voice in the darkness outside. "More of you off to the right. *Más aprisa!*"

Mike, once the pressure eased momentarily, snatched up the bayoneted rifle of a fallen Legionnaire and, bareheaded, joined the struggling mass in the gate tunnel. Subconsciously, he realized that the battle was now at that critical stage which would probably spell defeat for one side or the other.

Beyond the *képis* of the foremost Legionnaires, he could see a shifting throng of guerrillas, drawn up in a thick rank all the way across the great courtyard. They were firing steadily, and from the walls above their sharpshooters were also shooting down into the court.

The Legionnaires, bayonets redly a-gleam, doggedly kept on trying to win through the gate, but their attack was unmistakably losing momentum.

Despair seized Mike. God! The campaign which he had so carefully plotted was going astray. Carolina would soon be doubly lost.

Brave as the French were, human beings could not stand the rain of lead which was pouring on them, and as a fresh group of Legionnaires fell in a bloody welter, the men in blue and red halted, wavered, and in spite of their N.C.O.'s frantic calls, began to fall back.

"Defeat!—You've lost!" shrieked perverse, demoniac voices in Mike's soul. But at that moment a wild clatter of hoofs rang out. From corrals, which had been pulled down by Mike's Yaquis and *caçadores,* there burst a flood of fear-maddened horses. These, long terrified by the smoke and the sparks which had been raining on them during the past ten minutes, were quite crazed with fear. Snorting like steeds from Valhalla, they galloped wildly about.

IN A SHAGGY torrent they charged headlong across the vast courtyard, now slipping on the blood of the dead, now tripping on the shrieking wounded, and at last bumping into the rear of the guerrilla line, so throwing them out of position. Cursing, el Hiena's men snatched out their machetes and hamstrung the maddened brutes as fast as they could.

"Now we've got them.—*En avant! Adelante! Forward!*"

Seeing the disorder of the guerrillas, and feeling the slackening of that murderous fire, the invaders at last poured in through the gate and quickly formed a line inside.

"*Viva la República!*" Over the walls from outside Escandón's green-coated infantry now began to appear and made their machetes gleam like bright windmills of death.

Mike, sweat-bathed and gasping for breath, found himself on the right wing, firing at the struggling mass of bandits. His heart lifted when a Legion bugle's brazen voice shrieked a brief call. Down swept the long French bayonets, and with a heart-shaking cry of "*Vive l'Empereur!*" they charged, while behind them dismounted dragoons and the balance of the *caçadores* poured in through the gate to form a second line behind the Legionnaires.

At last Mike saw Andy. Outwardly cold and collected, he was skillfully directing the attack, using his dripping sword as a pointer.

All at once el Hiena's men lost their nerve. Shrieking in mortal terror, they broke and ran for the wall, scattering like a flock of chickens when a hawk hovers above. By tens and twenties they scaled the walls and dropped over.

"To bad to let 'em get away," Mike bawled to his brother.

"They won't," Andy shouted grimly: "Your *encurado* lancers are waiting for 'em outside."

10

BACK TO THE WARS

THROUGH THE DRIFTING acrid, blue smoke Andy bore down on his brother. Mike's face was black with powder, his uniform was ripped open, and a shallow cut on his gaunt left cheek was sending a trickle of blood dripping across his chin.

"For God's sake, where's Carolina?" he shouted, above the pitiful screaming of the hamstrung horses and the yells of the guerrillas who, cornered in various parts of the ruin, were now trying to buy their sordid lives.

Now and then, from outside the walls, rang the shriek of some wretch, speared by the lancers and *encurados* who circled outside like so many vigilant cats waiting for ferret-run rats to appear.

"Answer me, or I'll go crazy!—Have you seen Carolina?" repeated Andrew, dashing a smoke-blackened hand across his forehead.

"Not since the fight began," replied Mike. "Come along. The last I saw of her was down at that end—"

"God, if they've hurt her—!" choked Andy, a terrible light in his gray eyes.

Mike thought it wise to forbear any mention of the scene which he had beheld by the firelight.

"You don't know what it means," Andrew choked as they ranged back and forth, "to have thought Carolina lost, to have found her again—then to—"

He ducked to avoid a swirl of spark-laden smoke; and while Mike directed the efforts of some of his green-clad *caçadores* in forcing a doorway, Andrew called together a dozen of his Legionnaires, directing them to abandon all other effort in order to search for the missing girl.

Slowly the search took shape, as groups of terrified bandit women, together with their sullen masters, were herded at the bayonet point into the center of the court-yard.

Presently the various parties of searchers began to report. But none of them had seen a trace either of el Hiena or of the Señorita de Luria.

"Well, one thing's a cinch," growled the commander of the French forces, "they haven't gone outside the walls. So they must be here in the ruin somewhere."

It was then that one of the Yaquis who had accompanied Mike ran up, his oblique eyes lit with excitement.

"*Señor comandante,*" he panted. "Quick! Follow me. My brother struggles with three guerrillas."

"Where?" snapped Mike.

But the Yaqui had already turned and was bounding off to the left. Without an instant's delay, the brothers set off after him, full tilt. They found him in a ruined shrine, pointing to a spot where a couple of packing cases stood pulled aside to reveal the dark entrance of a shaft. It was down this that the Yaqui darted, his naked shoulders glimmering in the light of a brand which he snatched from a blazing *jacal.*

THE TUNNEL PROVED to be shallow, very short, and ending in a small, rock-walled chamber. In it a strange sight could be seen by the feeble light of a couple of gourd lamps. Two men were wrestling on the floor. One of them Mike instantly recognized as a Yaqui. He was locked in a death grip with a huge shirtless guerrilla, who strove to drive a dagger between the Indian's ribs. Intent above them towered the man who had wielded the whip over Carolina, and el Hiena, his evil mouth twisting and jerking more than ever. Just as the trio bounded across the threshold, the guerrilla tore his arm free and succeeded in plunging his knife into the side of that Yaqui who had struggled so valiantly against great odds.

Just a glimpse did the brethren catch of a pale, disheveled Carolina, crouched in a corner, her huge eyes round with horror as she clutched the tattered remains of the shawl in an ineffectual attempt to cover her nakedness.

In deadly silence, the six men flew at each other, Mike selecting the colossal man of the whip. Andy took el Hiena; the Yaqui his kinsman's murderer.

It was a fantastic, nightmarish sort of struggle that ensued by the amber light of the flickering gourd lanterns. It was a question of who could most efficiently use knife or fist, for the space was too limited to admit the use of pistols.

"Andrew! Mike! Save me!" Choked and desperate was Carolina's appeal.

Above the panting combatants a hideous Aztec god leered down as though pleased to see human blood spilt at his feet once more.

The struggle was as brief as it was fierce, since the three marauders were no match for a trio burning with a white-hot sense of outrage. The guerrilla, already weakened by the dead Yaqui's knife thrust, was the first to go down, with the avenger's knife point buried in the throat, just beneath his ear. Next, Mike's clubbed pistol took his yellow-featured enemy of the whip between his small, evil eyes.

A fraction of an instant later, Andrew's fist impacted squarely upon el Hiena's jaw with a *smack* that rang loud in the little shrine; and the outlaw chief reeled backwards, to strike his head against the feet of the stone idol. Uttering a brief, strangled gasp, he flung his jewelled hands towards the smoky ceiling and fell senseless, thus affording a prime candidate for the gallows.

"Andrew! Mike!" Swaying, forgetful of her disarray, Carolina arose totteringly, the sheen of her white body gilded by the gourd lamps. First she fixed her glorious eyes on the older and then on the younger brother—?

"Mis hermanos! Ah! Never had I thought to see you again."

"Thank God! Thank God!" was all Andrew could gasp as he snatched a gay *zerape* from a nail driven into the wall, and flung it about Carolina's smooth white shoulders.

"Ah, I am doubly happy!" she sobbed. "First, that you came in time, second that you fight side by side, and not one against the other. Help me, please—I—I am very tired."

AS THEY LED her forth from the sinister presence of the Aztec idol, both brothers were silent, suddenly aware that with the passing of another day their strange armistice must end. Once more, they must become bitter enemies— officers who must obey orders. But of that they said nothing to Carolina de Luria.

The sun climbed high in a brazen sky before the joint expedition completed its work at the ruin. All morning long, group after group of those human tigers who, under el Hiena, had scourged Oaxaca for the last five years faced the tireless firing squads. Some died bravely screeching obscene defiance at their executioners; others wept and slobbered for the mercy they had denied others. But all died.

Last of all, the punitive expedition hanged the arch-villain el Hiena, together with his lieutenant, the wielder of the whip, from that same gateway which had been so dearly won. A deep sigh arose from the assembled troops as el Hiena's body at last dangled quite still.

"The *aldeanos* will sleep better now," they murmured.

Then the expedition, having loaded their wounded on such of the bandits' horses as had not been hamstrung or destroyed by fire, set off from that forbidding ruin over which thick flocks of crows and buzzards were already circling in anticipation.

"*Qué hay?*" demanded Carolina. "Why do you two ride like a pair of mummies? Have you not won? Have you not rid the world of an evil monster? Smile then!"

Once more her bright and cheerful self, and bewitchingly mannish in a rich man's bolero and a pair of silver mounted breeches selected from the loot, the heiress of the de Lurias turned from one to the other of the somber-faced brothers.

Mike forced a smile and raised his eyes from the sunburnt grass slipping by under el Aquila's dainty hoofs. "Oh, I reckon Andy's thinking about the men he's lost— over a hundred. But at that rate, I should look even sadder;

I've got a hundred and thirty-five killed, wounded and missing. It cost me something to take that blasted ruin!"

"Sure, that's it—" Andy began, but at length he raised unhappy eyes. "It's no use, Mike, I can't pretend any longer."

"Pretend?" A look of pained surprise crept into Carolina's dark eyes. "What is wrong? Am I not safe? Are you not allies?"

"We were, little sister," explained Mike gently. "But very soon we shall have to separate and take up the war again—just where we left off."

CAROLINA'S SLIM BODY shook as under a blow, and she stared incredulously from the man in red to him in blue.

"Oh, *Dios, Dios!* Then it is true?—But you cannot do this! God forbids such wickedness! Are men mad that they must fight whenever they disagree?"

Fiercely she pleaded, first with Andrew and then with Mike.

"No, Carolina, dear," said Mike in a hopeless monotone. "We've got to play the game as gentlemen play it. Look here, when we separate you'd better go along with Andy. Your plantation may have been sacked, along with ours. You'll be safe with the French. Our armistice lasts until sunrise and then—*quién sabe?*" He spread his hands with a sad effort at gaiety.

But Carolina only wept.

Late in the afternoon, Lieutenant Escandón urged his rangy bay up alongside and said:

"*Por Dios,* major. All day have I awaited your orders. Now I must ask for them. What do you intend? You know, there are not two hundred cartridges left among our forces? The ammunition which we hoped to recover was burnt."

But even now, Mike did not seem ready to face the problem presented by the future. Puzzled, the young Mexican aristocrat followed his commander's absent gaze, and found it fixed on a range of bare, brown hills lying far off to the left.

"Why," he inquired with well-bred patience, "why do you day-dream like this? Surely you must know there is no help coming from Conino? All day long you have looked as though you expected to see reënforcements coming, and God knows General Juarez has not a man to—"

WITH SURPRISING SPEED Mike aroused himself from his lethargy and clapped a hand over the *caçadore* officer's mouth.

"Silence!" he hissed, blue eyes very intent beneath the shako visor, "I want you to talk about our cavalry, our splendid *encurados,* our superb dragoons from Guanajato. *Entiende!* Speak so that the French commander can hear without realizing that you are talking for his benefit."

"But," Escandón's very black eyes were eloquent with despair, "that would be useless. We have no such cavalry—a troop of dragoons, maybe, at Conino. Mere talk will not frighten this terrible brother of yours. He will advance on the fords to-morrow morning. I know him now. *Sí,* his legionnaires will attack, and then we die. Think well, *comandante*—think well before you doom us all to death."

"My brother may not be frightened," was Mike's strange reply as Escandón rode off with a bitter laugh, "but others may be. Good God, if only I knew whether those gallopers got through yesterday—Sergeant!" he beckoned Lieutenant Spurr up alongside, "how many cattle did we have down in the Novedad valley?"

"About five thousand head, sir—prime long horn beeves."

"Um," Mike nodded, and was mimicked by his shadow, blue-black on the hot earth. "And you really think those messengers got through?"

"They're the best scouts hereabouts. Yep, you can bet your sombrero that General Juarez got your despatch last night, 'bout the same time we was tanglin' up with them *mal hombres* back yonder."

"And the note to Station Number One?"

"Told Luke to give it to Frank Baldwin. Frank's onery as a cow with a new calf, but he'll follow orders 'spite hell, high water or congress." The Texan's bright black eyes narrowed and he rode closer. " 'Scuse my askin', sir, but what in hell do you want with them beef critters?"

A bleak smile passed over Mike's hot, red face. "I'm trying to keep from killing my brother, or have him kill me. You'll agree there's not much fun in either situation?"

"So long as he's set to take that there ford, and you're jest as set to stop him, don't see how you can help it," replied the Texan, shaking his narrow head. "Wal, mebbe when we reach the heights of San Gabriel we'll see a way out."

"Maybe. Keep a sharp lookout towards the west—tell the Yaquis, too. They can see a field mouse scratching its ear a mile away."

Taking a canteen from his pommel, Mike drew a long draught of tepid water, for the sun was hot and he was weary with that weariness familiar only to veteran soldiers. **SOON THE HEIGHTS** of San Gabriel loomed ahead, three low hills crowned with dead trees on which flocks of buzzards roosted. It was then that Mike, with a muttered excuse to Andy and the tragic-eyed girl riding numbly by his side, cantered ahead, ostensibly to study the San Gorgio valley which, in all its lush richness, lay spread out below like an unrolled chart.

Like a sculptured rider the young brother sat his saddle, again and again sweeping the terrain below with infinite care, as though his soul's salvation lay yonder. At last, with a face that had become wan, haggard and strangely aged, he turned and fell in at his place at the head of the column.

By one of those strange paradoxes that make war the sardonic thing it is, on that last night of their armistice the two forces made camp together above the ford that would soon run red with their mutual blood. The bronzed Legionnaires drank hugely of the fiery *tequila* and *pulque* which the little brown *soldados* of the Republic offered to them; and, not to be outdone, they made free with their own white bread, red issue wine, and rank but aromatic tobacco.

While dusk settled, dragoons, *encurados* and Imperialist cavalrymen mingled in jovial camaraderie; and when some of the German Legionnaires lifted their magnificent voices in the plaintive *liebeslieder,* the swarthy and bronzed groups about the smouldering camp fires fell silent.

But there was neither mirth nor conviviality in the officers' tents. Talking and smiling mechanically, sat Carolina, with one of the brothers on either side. Captain Zapatos, his empty sleeve dangling limp because of a wounded shoulder, sat frowning into space as he mused on the morrow.

Lieutenant Escandón played listlessly at picquet with Lieutenant La Marche; and it was the French lieutenant, alone of all that assemblage, who seemed comparatively light-hearted. But even he had his silent moments whenever he read the suppressed anguish on the faces of that trio sitting a little to one side and staring out at the bivouac.

"Surely," Carolina was saying for the hundredth time, "you will not, cannot, commit this criminal folly? Duty has no right to make men demons—"

"We have no choice," Mike said. "Soldiers must obey orders. And so, when dawn comes, I am going to march my force across the San Gorgio—"

"And then—you—you'll retreat?" How fervent was the plea in Carolina's eyes. "Ah, dear God!—Say, promise, that you'll retreat? Give me my Andrew, Mike dear. You know how I love him—he is everything in the world to me.— And you come next!"

"NO, DEAR CAROLINA. I'll halt on the other bank—and take up a defensive position."

"And very soon after that," Andrew added with downcast eyes, "I shall attack. You see, little Carolina, it doesn't interest General Lorençez at all that I'm fighting my own flesh and blood—that I'll have to hang Mike and Escandón and Spurr and the rest if I capture them. To Lorençez it's only a question of capturing this important ford. All he cares about is whether it's held—or not held. General Méjia is so damned scared of an attack on our flank that he wants this whole valley made safe."

And as Andy said that, Escandón glimpsed Mike's eyes flickering upwards a brief instant.

"Well, Bud, he's got good reason!" observed Mike suddenly. "His flank isn't safe. Did you see that Indian ride up to me this afternoon?"

Every head in the tent turned to face the speaker.

"Yes. What of it?"

"Well, he was telling me that six thousand Guanajato dragoons, after making forced marches, had at last joined our main army."

To this the man in blue uttered a strident laugh and beat his fists together gently. "You lie like a gentleman, Mike! But there's no use bluffing. We've a swarm of reliable spies at your headquarters. Not a squad of *peons* joins your outfit that we don't know of the next day—or the day before, maybe. Six thousand dragoons?"

From the shadows Lieutenant La Marche uttered a mirthless laugh. "Six thousand cows, more likely. I hope, Major Lockheed, that your staff won't try anything so silly as driving cattle to make General Méjia think they're cavalry."

"Of course not!" said Escandón, hurriedly.

Inexorably, La Marche went on. "Any idiot can tell when a dust cloud is caused by cavalry or cattle. You see, my dear lieutenant, cattle don't wear bridles, nor do they have riders who carry sabers which sparkle and shine in the sun."

A close observer might have noticed that Mike's big hands twitched just a fraction of an inch as he heard that. But, forcing a smile to his sun-cracked lips, he said:

"We'd never try to fool an old campaigner like General Méjia. He's seen too many cattle and too many cavalry— at a distance."

Again the conversation languished, until at last Carolina vented a weary sigh, got up, and taking the brothers by the hands led them out of the tent and into the clean, blue-white starlight which shed a delicate radiance over plain, mountain and stream.

"Your minds are made up, I see," she said in a low but firm voice. "And I, too, have made my mind up. Don Mike," she turned toward him the pale oval of her face, which in its distress was lovelier than Mike could ever recall having seen it, "I—I'm going to stay in Andrew's camp."

"Fine," said the younger brother heartily, "I'd hoped you would, Carolina. Now, there's no use being silly about all this."

BUT THE STARS shimmered on the Spanish girl's glossy head when she shook it gently. "I stay because I am already through the French lines. I—I will never return to the San Gorgio country again. If—if Andrew dies, I shall mourn his memory in a convent beyond the sea. If you die, dear Mike, I swear I will never marry the man whose hands are red with your blood.—Perhaps that," she said with a flare of anger, "will bring you two to your senses." So saying, she hurried off in the darkness to her tent, leaving the unhappy brothers to face the longest night that either of them had ever known.

All night long the two sat by a small, yellow-flickering fire, talking of the happy days that had been; of the hours they had spent in childhood, trapping rabbits and shooting at coyotes, of their father, that upright, sternly kind old man; of a thousand other nearly forgotten episodes.

The stars rolled on in their courses and a moon, paler and smaller than it had been the night before, cast a feeble radiance on the two armies. Within a few hours those armies would be flinging themselves upon each other.

Long they listened to the mournfully musical *"Centinela*

alerta-a-a!" of Mike's sentries; to the eerie wail of a coyote; to the deep-toned snoring of the Legionnaires, those men from the other side of the world.

At last the eastern sky paled, and Mike, shivering a little in the cold predawn wind, got up.

"Good-bye, Andy," he said. "And—and good luck. If I lose, I promise that you won't take me alive. Carolina will never be able to blame you for my death."

"And I—I won't live to take you prisoner, Bud." Andrew's face was quivering. "Oh God!" he cried fiercely. "We can't—we can't do this. I—I'll go back to Lorençez, tell him I refuse to obey."

"And get shot for insubordination in the face of the enemy," reminded Mike gently. "No, it wouldn't do any good. Your general would only send some one else, some one whom I'd have to fight. And there's Carolina, too, you see.—It's got to be done. Good-bye, Bud."

Neither could look at the other as they clasped hands. Then Mike, still feeling the warmth of Andy's hand on his fingers, rode over to his part of the bivouac and briefly ordered his buglers to blow the reveille.

11

DRAGOONS!

AGAIN THE PLOVERS whistled as they ran with brisk little steps along the silvery sands of the fords of San Gorgio. Again the quail began to call to each other, and again the tops of the Santa Lucrezia mountains grew rosy. But Mike saw none of these things. For the first time in his life he cursed the frightened *soldados* as he ordered them into position.

"Courage is good, but this—Name of God, this is suicide," protested Zapatos fiercely. "Half of the men have no bayonets. There is not ammunition enough for more than one volley. *Por piedad,* order a retreat!"

"We must stay," said Mike stiffly. "Obey orders, captain, always obey orders. That's the motto which makes a good army and wins the battles."

How cool that dawn wind was. How often he had sniffed its perfumed sweetness, and now it was for the last time! Yes, this would very likely be the last time he would see the sun lift above those familiar, ragged peaks on the horizon.

"More men to the center, dammit!" he roared. "What's the matter with you, Spurr? Throw a squad in behind that row of rocks."

"Yes, sir," replied Spurr, his narrow eyes a-gleam with the

prospect of battle. He scrambled down towards the river bed with a group of frightened-looking *caçadores* shambling at his heels.

Over Mike crept a great sense of futility, of helplessness, above all, of weariness. He had struggled and fought to prevent this enormous trick which Fate had played on him and his brother. He had gambled and had won the minor stakes, only to lose in the last and vital turn of the game. He shivered in the keen air, and drew himself up very straight. On the other bank the Legionnaires were falling in, their solid ranks of red pantaloons weaving a bright, restless design. Out on their flanks the red and green Imperial Lancers were commencing to pull the gayly fluttering pennons from their lance tips, in preparation for the grim work ahead.

God, if he only had some ammunition it would be a cinch to hold that ford! But he hadn't. Looking more and more like a desperate young Mars, Mike strode back and forth, haunted eyes ever reverting to the eastward.

"*Oíga! Señor comandante!* A messenger!" Half a hundred eager voices called out.

AN IMPERIAL LANCER, with a white flag snapping at his lance head, was cantering down to the misty water. Now he was in, and splashing across to hail the red-clad commander of the Republican army.

"For the last time, *señor, el Capitán* Lockheed begs you to surrender, for the sake of the men under your command."

A sudden resolution shook the redheaded officer's being. It was not right to lay down these men's lives. He would surrender. Yes, by God, he would!—But even as he opened his mouth there rang in his ears the deep voice of his father, "Obey orders, my son, always obey orders!"

There was no doubt that General Juarez, that desperate, oft-betrayed Indian patriot, had ordered him to hold the fords to the last man. He shook his head.

"*Gracias*. Please tell Captain Lockheed we will defend the ford."

Solemnly, the lancer dipped his lance in salute, then wheeled and splashed back across the ford.

"No one is to fire until I give the word," Mike shouted, and his heart sank when he saw how few of his men made any attempt to adjust their sights. A few were hopelessly locking their bayonets in place. Poor devils! They weren't cowards, these Mexicans, for cowards would never sit there with empty guns waiting for the scythe of doom to mow them down.

On the other bank a bugle shrilled, sounding the advance. The blue ranks stirred, began to move, long bayonets gleaming in the light of the newly risen sun.

Poor Carolina! She must be dying a hundred deaths. And Mike's anguish increased as he made out his brother Andrew, well out in front of his men. He was riding slowly down to the river, the scarlet top of his *képi* glowing bright red. Stiffly, like an automaton, he rode; his rawboned black mare slipping a little as she neared the water's edge.

Clump! Cr-r-unch! Clump! The tramp of those hobnailed feet on the other side of the river sounded loud. Mike could see Lieutenant La Marche, his eyeglasses gleaming faintly, as with a drawn sword he directed the movement.

FORWARD RODE ANDREW, neither sword nor pistol in his gauntleted hand. But his head was up and his eyes were fixed on the red figure of his brother, standing outlined on the bank above, an easy target for the first Legion volley.

Now Andrew's horse was taking to the water, sending spray up on the rider's knee boots.

"Ready!" cried Mike, his voice hoarse. A few musket locks *clacked*. "Aim!" How horrible to think that Andrew—with everything to live for—would in an instant tumble into that swift current, robbed of all his pulsing life. Among the rearmost Imperial Lancers there arose a shout.

"Para! Para!—Halt! A messenger!"

Mike's red-clad figure relaxed while he watched Andy halt his mare. Down the far bank came sliding a gorgeous, yellow-clad Hussar galloper. He thrust into Andy's hand a dispatch.

Through his glasses Mike watched his brother read the missive, saw that set frown disappear from Andy's face, and a smile twitch the corners of his mouth. This expression was then in turn replaced by an expression of amazed incredulity.

Facing his men, the Legion officer gave an order which presently sent them scrambling back up that bank which they had descended only a moment before. Then Andrew signalled for parley.

"Come on, sergeant." Mike, grinning from ear to ear, flung himself on El Aquila and cantered out into the stream.

"What is it, Bud?" he inquired. "Get cold feet?"

Andy grinned. "No, damn the luck! Something's always spoiling our fun. Just got a frantic dispatch from Méjia ordering my instant return to the main column. He must be crazy! He said a big cavalry force has appeared and threatens our communications."

"Ah, yes!" said Mike. "Those will be the Guanajato dragoons."

"Dragoons, your grandmother!" snapped Andy. "I know damn well Juarez hasn't more than a troop of cavalry to his name. A reliable spy told me so last night. He never lies to me."

"And yet Méjia is a good general," quoth Mike, wiping drops of sweat from his brow. "Maybe if we go to that hilltop we can see what's happened."

SIDE BY SIDE, they cantered to the hill and halted there, to be gilded by the sunrise. Out came glasses.

"There they are, sir," Spurr said, pointing far to the east. "Look at 'em, will you?"

In silence, Andy, Mike and La Marche studied that distant pall of dust near the head of which could be distinguished row on row of very distant cavalry.

"Must be a whole brigade," cried Escandón. *"Viva la República!"*

All the observers saw that it was indeed a huge pillar of dust; moreover, that from the center of the dust cloud the morning sun drew innumerable sparks of fire such as never shone from dusty cattle. Straggling behind were more dragoons, evidently mounted on sick and feeble horses.

"We must leave at once," said Lieutenant La Marche, excitedly. "Those are not cattle. The flash of breastplates and the gleam of the helmets are there."

"It's cavalry, all right," said Andy with a slow smile. "Compared to you, Bud, Napoleon was a rookie. And some time very soon Carolina and I will name our eldest after you."

"*Mon Dieu!*" La Marche protested. "You are wasting time, captain. That cavalry will cut us off in a half hour!"

Once more the hard, brown hands of the brethren clasped, then Mike wheeled and recrossed the river.

"All right, sergeant," he said, "call in the men. We'll go back to Las Estrellas and try to clean up the mess there. Then I'm going to show you something."

"Yes?" grinned Spurr. "I expect you're going to show me a brigade of dragoons. Where in hell did you get 'em?"

"From up my sleeve.—Here, you lancers! Get in column!"

Though thoroughly sacked, the ranch was yet in reparable condition.

When the sun had just begun its downward course, that tall column of dust came very near to Las Estrellas.

Mike rode out to meet it.

But it was not a brigade of cavalry that he reviewed— only a single hot and dusty troop of dragoons who were herding along some five thousand long-horned cattle which were lowing thirstily. The horns of the big steers were decked with the weirdest assortments of ornaments imaginable. The great herd shuffled past, ever and anon shaking their heads and making the sun play on belt buckles, forks, knives, spoons, mirrors—in fact anything that could cause a glitter. But the objects were very tightly lashed to the horns of the rightful tenants of Las Estrellas.

Slowly a big, bronze-helmeted captain of dragoons rode up to Mike and saluted gravely. "*Bueno?*" he inquired.

"*Bueno,*" replied Mike with a grin.

THE SNARING OF
SERGEANT FROST

*A firing squad promises a pleasanter
death than the fate of a Legion spy
caught in Touareg territory*

1

A FEUD IS RENEWED

SERGEANT LEMUEL ZEBULON FROST tilted back his gaunt, sunburned head the better to permit a graceful parabola of the fiery red Sudanese wine to spurt from a battered earthenware jug into his narrow mouth. As his admiring companion noticed, his Adam's apple remained quite still and he made no effort to swallow, having long since mastered that technique of the beer drinker who opens certain muscles of the throat and pours the liquid in.

Not a foot above the worthy sergeant's black head swung a malodorous butterfat lamp that, like others set in niches cut into the tavern's stone walls, imperfectly revealed the drinker's rugged and Indian-like profile, and a nose which, though originally straight and well formed, had become battered and dented during years of turbulent living. Below this noble ruin a powerful, narrow jaw jutted out to reveal a long purple scar running along its left side.

"Boy baby, that sure made a three point landing!" sighed the drinker, deftly wiping his lips on the dusty cuff of a heavy dark blue overcoat. "Hear that there hog-wash they calls wine sizzle over the tiles, Bud?"

Across the small, food spotted wooden table the second Legionnaire, a short, little man with pointed features unex-

The inn became a bedlam of fighting men.

pectedly emerging from a flat background of a face, set down his jug and grinned a gold spangled grin.

"S'elpme, Lem, 'arf a litre at one slug," he sighed. "Does yer breathe through yer ears? Better go slower though or yer'll be 'avin' the blinkin' sour-belly."

"Not on this pale pink slop," grunted the sergeant, restlessly shifting his angular frame on the greasy cushion beneath him. With frank disapproval he studied the tavern of the Three Pale Moons which, of Agadés's limited—and sternly prohibited—supply of resorts, had seemed to offer the greatest promise of surcease from the cares of a Legionnaire's existence.

On all sides of the two blue and white clad Legionnaires crouched perhaps forty natives with hawk-profiled brown faces, with small muscular hands and cavernous black eyes that were never still. Through shifting strata of tobacco smoke Lemuel glimpsed two other members of the expeditionary force in the guise of a brace of swaggering, quick

"Stop 'em!" implored Lem, still hoping to avert disaster.

gestured Spahis, whose white burnooses and red revers shone brightly amid the sour smelling gloom. They seemed ill at ease for all their nonchalance, and talked with a great show of white teeth and kept glancing at a small stage at the far end of the room.

"Gawd, but it's thick," complained Lemuel. "If this here honky-tonk ever does stir in its sleep we won't be able to see no cooch dancers from here."

The room, which measured perhaps twenty by thirty feet, was unprepossessing even for a desert town of the lower Sahara. The air was foul with the reek of cheap wine and stank of bodies for weeks unwashed and of the accumulated dust of years, for Agadés lies as Lemuel frequently and profanely remarked, not more than a spit and short jump above the equator. Moreover, it is a very old town— perhaps too old—for the first bricks of its walls had been laid by Nubian refugees out of Egypt, many centuries before the upper Niger region was described on the maps of the world as La Territoire Militaire Du Haut Niger. Better had it been described as the territory of Blood, Thirst and Cruelty.

Even to the travel-blasé Legionnaires of the Sixième Compagnie, Agadés had presented something new. Incredulously they had stared when its machicolated, red-brown towers had reared themselves above the blinding heat of the desert.

"Wal, may I be a long, tall son of a buzzard," Lemuel had exclaimed when the Legion's chase of Shereef Ayoub Behar had brought it to the stokehold heat of Agadés, "if that there burg don't look like a bunch of skyscrapers!"

"Nah," Corporal 'Arold 'Ackbutt had objected. "Looks more like a blinkin' rabbit warren wiv orl them 'ouses piled one on top of the other."

But neither towering walls of sun-dried brick, nor a numerical advantage of four to one had persuaded the wily Ayoub, Shereef of all the Kidal Touaregs, that it was yet time to halt and to try conclusions with the weary Legionnaires in that doggedly plodding blue and white column. No, better retreat on into the maddening, heat-blasted wastes of el Kidal until the arrival of certain faithful vassals increased the odds to at least ten to one. And so the worthy Ayoub, falling back, had delivered weary old Agadés into the hands of the accursed Roumis.*

A GANGLING FULA slave boy shambled up with a soft scuffing of bare feet and, from a bloated goat skin, replenished the jug Lemuel held forth in a bronzed and tattooed hand.

---

* Roumis—white men. Originally Romans.

"Fill her up, Bub," he rumbled, "and help slake down the biggest thirst that's been growed since the Armistice. Jeeze, Bud, I got enough dust in my gills to start a Swiss farm."

In from the narrow and crooked street outside the tavern's stout wooden door drifted a snatch of song. It was the familiar *"Tiens, voilà du Boudin!"* roared out by deep, Nordic voices.

The native patrons squirmed restlessly in their dirty white *gandouras*, glowered and bent further over their tiny cups of thick, dark brown coffee.

"Some more of the boys off duty," Lemuel pronounced as he relaxed. "Thought it was a patrol, maybe. Reckon that means Ahmadu's gang o' cutthroats has pulled safe into camp."

'Arold swallowed a deep gulp of the bitter Sudanese wine and smiled happily. "Ahmadu? 'O's 'e?"

Before replying, Lemuel undid the three top buttons of his dusty tunic and fixed on his sunburned companion a look of mingled pity and distaste.

"Don't you never learn nothing? Don't you never keep them gummy lop-ears o' yours open for nothing but 'soupy' and the pop of the cork? Ain't you heard this Ahmadu is a big buddy of ourn?"

"No—wot for? Why should 'e love the Frenchies?"

"Brer Ahmadu aims to be boss of all the Kidal Touaregs; so he's quit old Ayoub cold."

"Ow!" In the uncertain light of the lamps, the cockney's wine-flushed features lit. "So 'e's a blinkin' renegade?"

"Sure." Lemuel's dark, close cropped head inclined. "What with Ahmadu's gang, the four airplanes and those platoons o' the Seventh that pulled in, I feel a leetle mite

easier. We'll have all of five hundred men and better reconnaissance.

"Yep, planes come in darned handy in this blasted stokehold of a country—but I'd hate to fly one and be forced
down near a Touareg *douar*. Reckon I'd give myself a slug
between the eyes, 'cause these natives make Apaches look
rank amatoorish when it comes to torture."

'Arold cursed a fat slattern who tried to fondle his chin.
All in one breath he went on. "No, Lemuel, I don't like the
wye this blinkin' campaign is goin'. Them Touaregs with
their veiled fyces and narsty 'abits is a 'ard lot. Did yer see
wot we found o' Willie McKenzie this afternoon?"

The gaunt American settled back on his cushion, frowning absently at certain quaint and distressingly obscene
frescoes on the wall opposite. "I'd like to get a crack at them
mal hombres. But, what the hell? We can't live forever."

"—*La France est votre mère.*" As the singers in the street
outside brought their song to an end they applied heavy
boots to the battered wooden portal of the Inn of the Three
Moons.

"Enter with Allah." The proprietor, an enormous Hausa
Negro with shoulders and a belly that quivered like jelly
beneath his food spotted robes, waddled forward and drew
back sundry iron bolts. In the gloom beyond the doorway
three uniformed figures stood revealed.

Lemuel could glimpse a few stars shining behind them.

"Any Legionnaires in here?" The foremost Legionnaire,
a fox featured Spaniard, cautiously thrust head and shoulders inside the door and coughed as he peered through the
eddying smoke.

"Yer right, 'e's out o' the Seventh," remarked 'Arold to his companion. " 'E ain't none o' our crowd."

"Any Legionnaires?" demanded the second newcomer.

"Who in hell wants to know?" called Lemuel, amiably truculent. *"Alléz!* fish me the camp.* You boys run along home to the dear old Seventh—this ain't no kindergarten."

RESENTFUL DARK FACES shaded by djellaba hoods turned, and more than one of the tavern's patrons spat in the direction of the doorway.

"This honor is too great for my poor house," the landlord whined in a strange mixture of Arabic and French lingo.

"Sure, ye pot-bellied sister-seller, it's a stinkin' hole yez have here but we'll honor it." It was the third man who spoke now.

At the sound of that voice Lemuel started as though a Touareg lance had penetrated his blue-clad back. His hands gripped the scarred edges of the little table, his breath came in with a gentle hissing sound and, by the feeble amber rays of the lamps, 'Arold could see the skin over the American sergeant's naturally prominent cheek bones drawing tighter and tigher. Mystified, the cockney squirmed about on his yielding cushion to view the figure now filling the doorway.

" 'Ello," he remarked, in clearly audible tones, "strike me pink if it ain't a snotty nosed little aviator come to watch a real war—Wot's the matter, Flight Sergeant, did they clean up the *bordellos* of Timbuktu?"

He broke off short when Lemuel's hard hand closed over his wrist. "By the Lord," he muttered in that danger-

---

* *"Fiches moi le camp"*—liberally translated, "Get the hell out of here!"

ously soft voice which 'Arold knew and feared. "—By the Lord—if this ain't my lucky night!"

Cold gray eyes agleam, the Legion sergeant sat quite still while the two strange Legionnaires, with sword bayonets slatting on their hips, swaggered farther into the den, followed immediately by the blue-clad aviator.

The Agadéans, hissing dreadfully earnest curses, drew aside their burnoose skirts and called on Allah to blight these insolent *ferenghis*.

"Well, if it ain't the Chileno-Irishman," Lemuel said in clear, penetrating tones. "Glad to see you, Obregon, or is it O'Brien, now?"

"Obregon!" 'Arold's pinched features were desperately anxious as he reached across the table and seized his friend's right fist with both of his. "Steady, Lem, fer Gawd's sake. Don't start no rough 'ouse 'ere! It's three weeks *peloton punis* if we get caught off bounds."

With the slow certainty of a draw-bridge's rise, Lem's tall figure got to its feet and his head bent a little to avoid the lamp.

"Sit down! Sit down!" chattered 'Arold. "You can get at 'im better later on—"

But the shorter Legionnaire's pleas were vain. Like a fox terrier clinging to the leg of an enraged bull, he was dragged after Lemuel as that individual started forward, a grim smile on his lips.

"Better get ready, Tim Obregon." The American sergeant's voice was gritty, like the rasp of a file on an iron bar. "Yep—it's me, so you'd better get up on your hind legs, you treacherous rat!"

"Lem Frost! *Dios!* You are very hard to get rid of—" The

flight sergeant's heavy black brows met in a single puzzled line as he scrambled to his feet and towered, a powerful figure in light blue, quite as big as the hard bitten sergeant of the Legion.

"Keep your fat fingers out o' the soup," snarled Obregon, black eyes alight, when the Legionnaires of the *Septième Compagnie* would have backed him up. "Guess I'll have to fix this guy again, like I've fixed him before."

Reared in a land where violence and death are events as common as eating and sleeping, the patrons of the café calmly prepared to enjoy subsequent events in their own particular way. Snarling derisive advice over their shoulders, cruel featured Tukulas with tattooed foreheads and short forked beards and more delicately formed Rumas, drew daggers, yataghans and other interesting cutlery before retreating to line the walls.

THE TWO SPAHIS deftly and methodically upset their table amid a crash of broken pottery and crouched behind it, holding their service revolvers in generously beringed hands.

"Well, if yer will 'ave it out—"

Resigning himself to the inevitable, 'Arold drew his bayonet with a soft rushing *zwe-e-e-p!* and stood valiantly ready in the interests of fair play.

"Allah!" wailed the Hausa innkeeper, his yellow eyeballs rolling, "will no one stop these mad Roumis from ruining me?"

"Stand up and fight, ye half-caste mick!" growled Lemuel, his lips becoming tight, colorless creases in his bronzed features. "Seven years I been lookin' forward to this."

"I fear you not at all," snapped the flight sergeant as a dull red tide surged into the olive hued features, inherited from his Chilean mother. With his powerful right hand he sent a table flying, but as it crashed over he snatched a bottle from its top, expertly knocked its bottom off against the wall and, with the jagged neck clutched in his fist, sprang at the lanky American, loudly announcing his intentions of spilling that worthy's eyeballs on the refuse littered floor.

Lemuel's long body contracted and he balanced on the balls of his feet when that jagged end of the bottle flashed towards his face. With lightning speed his palms met in a thunderous clap, then flew violently apart, as though propelled by springs. Involuntarily the attacker's eyes followed the motion for a split fraction of a second. That flicker of time was enough, however, for Lem's right foot flashed up, caught Flight Sergeant Obregon's right wrist a shrewd kick and so numbed it that the jagged bottle flew far across the inn.

Amazed, the N.C.O. in light blue stared at his empty right hand, then his *képi* flew off and his heavy, evilly handsome head snapped violently back, because Sergeant Frost's horny right fist had landed on the point of his jaw. Venting a queer little grunt, the aviator swayed, then his knees suddenly went out from under him as though an unseen wire had jerked them forward.

Flushed and panting, Lemuel glared down at the sprawled form of his enemy; then he stirred the prostrate man with his heavy hobnailed foot.

"Get up, ye double crossing, left handed mick," he panted as he shook the hair out of his eyes. "I only begun—"

"Dios!" cried the Spanish Legionnaire, "you ask miracles, *mon sergent.* That blow would have knocked down a bull."

" 'E's out,' " Arold announced and sheathed his bayonet.

"Too damned bad," Lemuel said sorrowfully, as he kicked aside the litter of broken glass. "Reckon I'll wait for him to come to." Stooping, Lemuel caught the inert aviator by his collar and hauled him across the glass and pottery strewn floor to his table.

This done he sat down and banged on the wall. "Hey, *mozo,* let's have some more o' that bilge-water you call liquor. Come on over, boys," he waved a genial hand to the two new arrivals who remained standing in an unpleasant state of uncertainty. "We'll let that ornery son of a buzzard lie in the dirt where he belongs. What'll you have?"

Despite Lemuel's invitation, the Legionnaires from the Septième Compagnie remained across the room, but took great care to be polite in their refusal.

WITH VARYING DEGREES of rapidity the guests returned to their tables as, at the behest of the landlord, a bull fiddle began to squeak, while a Raita and a flute commenced to give forth a wailing air.

The cockney's sparrow-like visage loomed near through the swirling smoke.

"When did he tread so 'ard on yer precious little corns, Lem?"

Lemuel selected a cigarette from a very crushed package.

" 'Twas back in '23 durin' the Riff campaign. He was in the Legion then and in my platoon. We was both playin' the same dame—I really was nuts about her.

"One night when I was going on guard this ornery punk slips a paper o' chloral into my *jus.* I thought that java tasted kinda bitter at the time. Anyhow, I just about got to my post when the dope hit me and the sergeant o' the guard found me passed out. 'Course he turned me in for sleepin' on sentry-go."

'Arold's flat features pursed themselves in an expression of surprise and he regarded the prostrate aviator with new interest.

"Co-o-o! 'Ow come they didn't stand yer up before a wall?"

"They damned near did," said Lemuel, exhaling a small hurricane of blue smoke. "While I was bein' condemned to get the works this here son of a buzzard snags my gal." Over Lem's angular features flitted a reminiscent frown that boded ill for Sergeant Obregon. "I'd have got executed, too, if Willie McKenzie hadn't happened to keep the rest o' my coffee for a slug when I came off duty. They analyzed it and found I'd been doped, so I got off with six months chokey in the penal battalions.

"When I got back to the outfit this coyote," Lemuel's toe thrust the unconscious aviator's heavy, lax features into the rays of a lamp, "had been mustered out. I been looking for him ever since."

"Wot a yellow dog! Come on, let's get out o' 'ere afore somethink 'appens."

Lemuel's shadow, black and distorted on the dingy wall behind, mimicked the shaking of his head.

"No, we're stayin', and you're wrong about Obregon. This here guy's got enough Irish left in him to be a grade-A *soldado*. See that *Médaille Militaire* ribbon on his blouse? They don't give that out with no ham sandwiches, neither."

Lemuel's gray eyes grew suddenly direct and he faced the door. "What's that?" he asked sharply.

FROM BEYOND THE entrance sounded the indistinct trample of many feet and the murmur of voices. A patrol? All four Legionnaires stiffened and became warily alert.

Most of Lemuel's enjoyment faded when some one began hammering on the door—some one who pounded with the arrogant assurance of authority.

"W'allah! Cease thy uproar."

The landlord grumbled as, with a hoop of ponderous keys jangling over his leather apron, he again opened the door. This time, however, he uttered a brief gasp and stepped back, bending very low and whining some excuse.

"The Twareks!" Up sprang the diners, hands on weapons, while the music faltered, then died away.

Lemuel did not need to catch the murmur of "Ahmadu! Ahmadu!" to identify this evilly handsome personage who stood gazing truculently about.

Though not quite so tall as Lemuel, the Touareg chieftain was broader of shoulder, a fact emphasized by two cartridge belts which, crossing on his breast, bound in flowing robes of pale blue. To Tchek Ahmadu's wide leather belt was fastened a modern automatic, in sharp contrast to the other weapon which swung by the Touareg noble's side. This was a long, two handed sword, straight bladed and with a cross guard directly patterned on the type worn by crusaders to their conquest of the Holy Land.

While his followers entered, Tchek Ahmadu paused a moment, legs spread and small yellow-red hands on hips; of his face Lemuel could see very little for, like all Touaregs, this famed warrior's face was half veiled from above and below with a dark blue *litham*—a sort of thin blue muffler which covered his chin and his forehead, leaving visible only a narrow hooked nose and two piecing black eyes. As he paused, the Tchek idly fingered the hilt of a short dagger that was strapped to his left wrist.

"Narsty lookin' bloke," commented 'Arold with placid ignorance of this personage's importance. "Chuckin' 'is weight abaht and lookin' for trouble, shouldn't wonder."

The Touaregs remained silent, then a powerful warrior at Ahmadu's right spat loudly and remarked in guttural Arabic, "Continue to eat, swine."

"Enter with Allah, O mighty Tchek," whined the Hausa landlord.

"Pah! A jackal's den is cleaner!" Tchek Ahmadu's nose wrinkled in disgust as he advanced arrogantly into the tavern. Close at his heels strutted ten or eleven of the cruelest featured men Lemuel had ever beheld.

"So that's the bloke wot's goin' to fight on our side?" 'Arold demanded in a hoarse stage whisper. "Looks like a ruddy 'orse thief."

"Yes," agreed Lemuel. "I wouldn't trust him with a red-hot stove lid."

With a long, easy stride Ahmadu advanced arrogantly through the inn, treating the various patrons to contemptuous stares. When he drew near Lemuel's table both Legionnaires, out of respect to an ally, got up and stood to attention, whereat the other Legionnaires and the Spahis followed suit. Orders were orders, Lemuel firmly reminded himself. Steady gray eyes and truculent black ones met and clung in mutual appraisal.

JUST THEN FATE decreed that Tchek Ahmadu should trip

over the foot of Sergeant Obregon, lying quiescent in the shadows. The Touareg stumbled and fell to his knees amid a snicker of nervous amusement. Then, dignity outraged, he sprang up snarling furious curses.

"*Franzwazi* swine!"

His hand shot out and dealt the startled American sergeant a stinging slap on his lean brown cheek.

"Easy, sir—I didn't do that!"

Lemuel restrained his temper only because he was a soldier, first and above everything else. As such, he knew that to affront this valuable ally of France was no laughing matter; but when the Touareg spat in his face and started to draw his pistol, Lemuel saw death reaching out for him, and very naturally snatched at Ahmadu's pistol hand.

"Ai-e-e!" From the lesser Touaregs burst an incredulous and outraged gasp, and Murder, amid a sparkle of keen steel, leaped into the Inn of the Three Pale Moons. "Death to the *Franzwazis!*"

"Gawd, you've torn it now!" cried 'Arold and, ducking under a sword thrust, saw that Obregon's eyes were open again. There was, however, no time to think of anybody but himself. "Out, Lem—out!" On the top of a wooden stool the cockney caught the point of a yataghan aimed at Lemuel's back while he struggled to grasp Ahmadu's pistol hand. Though 'Arold could quite easily have reached the door at this juncture, he remained swinging the stool and clearing the way for Lemuel.

"Death to the *Franzwazis!*" The inn became a bedlam in which the Spahis and the two other Legionnaires were forced to fight for dear life as, by one accord, Agadéan and Touareg turned on the French.

"Stop it!" Lemuel yelled in Arabic. "Stop it!"

But Tchek Ahmadu's brown arms flashed clear of their loose sleeves and, black eyes terrible, he succeeded in jerking out his automatic.

Still hoping to avert the impending disaster, Lemuel at last succeeded in wrenching the pistol from Ahmadu's grasp.

"Make 'em stop," he panted. "Don't want no trouble."

"May ten thousand devils tear your soul!" screamed Ahmadu, squirming and clawing to reach his dagger.

"Stop 'em," implored Lemuel, who beheld a steel tipped wedge of blue veiled figures preparing to launch itself. "Talk to 'em—" So saying he interposed the renegade's body between his and the howling Touaregs.

"Come on!" With an elusive twist learned among the fish markets of Limehouse, 'Arold squirmed by Lemuel, just as Tchek Ahmadu's principal lieutenant aimed a hissing sword blow at Lemuel's head.

"Oh, you blasted fool!" Lemuel ducked with speed of the expert boxer he was, and so the bright blade missed him and instead bit deep into the neck of the Touareg chieftain.

"W'allah!" A shriek of mingled horror and rage went up when Ahmadu reeled in Lemuel's arms, bright arterial blood spurting over his white burnoose. The blue veiled bandits paused a moment in frozen amazement and that was a moment which Lemuel did not waste. He flew, rather than ran, out of the inn door and into the starlit night with the death shrieks of the butchered Spahis ringing in his ears.

"This wye, Lem!" 'Arold was calling urgently. "Quick! 'Ere they come!"

He darted off after that shadowy little figure while the town of Agadés awoke to take note of some of the liveliest minutes in its long, long history.

2

INTO THE DESERT

GREAT AND VARIED was the turmoil that ensued in Agadés when it became rumored that the mighty Ahmadu, Tchek of all the Arrerf Ahnet Touaregs, had been slain at the hands of a Legionnaire. Townfolk and countrymen became disapproving and distinctly nervous, in anticipation of reprisals by the merciless Forgotten of God. This disapproval displayed itself in showers of stones directed from housetops upon any and all French.

In the Legion's camp bugles brayed, drums beat and the whole expedition turned out all standing, which was fortunate for, amid the general alarm, Sergeant Frost and the cockney corporal were able, quite unnoticed, to rejoin their blasphemously annoyed platoon.

More bugles commenced sounding the *alerte* and, like the dead rising from their graves, Legionnaires appeared from the pup tents they had pitched on the hard dry soil of the *Territoire Militaire.*

"Gawd!" panted 'Arold, small eyes wide with fear. "The 'ole bloomin' camp's awake. It'll be our necks if they twig 'oo was in that shindy."

"Shut up," hissed Lemuel, sucking his bruised knuckles.

"I kin see that damned stone wall and firing squad already. But mebbe they won't find out.

"Here, turn out! Turn out!" he bawled as, reaching his own tent, he began to don his equipment.

"Wot'll we sye?" 'Arold queried while strapping his pack into place.

"We was just wandering around the town. Get me?" Lemuel said.

"Fat chance they'll believe that," was 'Arold's bitter comment. "We're jolly well in for it."

The upshot of it all was that, within twenty minutes of the moment Tchek Ahmadu had perished, the French camp was in arms and detachments were setting off for certain strategic points at the *pas gymnastique*.

Colonel Souchet's cold rage was terrible to behold, and Lemuel, standing in a silent double rank outside of headquarters, heard his voice.

"Find out who is responsible for this, Juarez. *'Cré nom de Dieu!* With the Arrerf Touaregs turned against us, this affair is like to cost us dear. Lieutenant Holvaag, who was the *misérable* responsible?"

"Two Legionnaires, it is said, sir," panted a young Swedish lieutenant who had just galloped down from the town.

"Legionnaires!" White mustaches aquiver, Colonel Souchet glared about while his staff joined in promising eternal damnation and sudden death to the wretches responsible. "So we have two stupid clods of Legionnaires to thank for the loss of the whole campaign.

"Captain Gonzales," he addressed a grizzled veteran with a silvery torpedo beard, "take three platoons of the

Sixième to the pass of el Dibella. Ahmadu's men should be far beyond it—they cannot yet have heard of this disaster.

"There you will dig some entrenchments and return half your force as soon as that is done."

During his long and tempestuous career Sergeant Lemuel Frost had felt depressed on many an occasion, but those past depressions were, as to his present despair, like plow furrows compared to the Grand Cañon. His back had become a race course for icy chills and, turning his eyes sidewise, he glimpsed sweat running in acid torrents over 'Arold's cheek.

"Nothin' to do but go on pump," * he told himself, "and the tooter the sweeter."

THE LITTLE PLAIN below Agadés's crumbling battlements now resounded to brief commands, to the clatter of rifles being brought to "inspection arms," and to the tread of several anxious little columns hurrying off into the menacing darkness.

Among the remaining three platoons of the Sixth Company the authors of the turmoil stood in gloomy silence. Why the devil couldn't they have been sent off—anywhere that was distant from Agadés?

In the morning a search was sure to be made and it was in no way encouraging to Lemuel that he heard the colonel offer a reward of four thousand *francs* for information leading to the arrest of the trouble makers.

"Four thousand *francs*—Gord 'elp us!" muttered 'Arold hopelessly. "Ain't a legendary in the 'ole bloomin' houtfit

---

* Go on pump—Legion slang for the act of deserting.

wot wouldn't eat 'is own child for a thousand *francs*. Yus, Lem, we've got to jolly well leg it."

"Reckon so," Lemuel admitted dolefully. "The signs say to make tracks. But still, there's a chance. Them two *hombres* outta the Seventh never got away. Reckon them Spahis got scragged, too, they was way inside—That leaves nothin' but natives to identify us, and even a court-martial thinks twice before condemning white men on the word of a A-rab."

In the starlight 'Arold's small eyes glinted as they sought Lemuel's.

"Ain't yer fergettin' about your friend Obregon? Just when the shindy begun I saw the blighter lying doggo under the tyble. Shouldn't wonder but 'e got away when the rest was a-chasin' us. The devil takes pertickler care o' his own, so they says."

"Obregon!" Lemuel stiffened. "Jeeze to Jenny, I clean forgot about that coyote! Yep, I'll bet that blasted two-timer got away, just like you say, and he sure will split his sides laughing when we sift lead.

"Steady, here come the orders."

A cadaverous looking *sous-lieutenant* was trotting across from the headquarters tent, hand steadying his sword, his hard face set in taut lines.

"*Garde à vous!*" Lemuel called his platoon to attention and then stiffened into an attentive ramrod.

"We move at once," Lieutenant Aymard announced crisply, "to cover the pass to the plateau of Yarda." He filled his lungs and throwing back his head called out, "By fours, forward, march!"

Simultaneously some hundred and fifty Legionnaires

shouldered arms and stepped off through the night with the starlight winking dully on the points of their long, four-edged bayonets.

It soon appeared that the detachment would skirt to the northward of the walls of Agadés when, in the darkness not far off to the right, a sudden crackle of rifle fire ripped the night silence to shreds.

"*Sapristi!* Volley fire!" Sergeant-major Pelletier, who marched beside Lemuel, glanced nervously off to the right. "Name of a name—! What does this mean, so near the camp? There can be none of the Shereef's men over there, and Tchek Ahmadu's rascals cannot yet have come up."

"Kinda looks like a surprise attack," remarked Lemuel, infinitely relieved to be off from Agadés and the danger of immediate discovery.

"Ah, name of Beelzebub!" remarked Pelletier, spitting viciously into the dusty caravan tracks, "—but I'd like to get my hands on the sacred gullets of the guilty ones. Four thousand *francs* isn't to be sneezed at. *Nom d'un pipe,* no!"

"No," agreed Lemuel with deep conviction, "it's not." AHEAD OF HIM he could catch the rise and fall of flat white *képi* tops, the flutter of the neck cloths, and the black outline of long Lebels swaying and stabbing at the great white stars above.

Reluctantly, he decided that if he and 'Arold wished to remain in good health there was no alternative to going on pump—a very risky proceeding in a territory so thoroughly barren and hostile. Let but one of the Legion's many enemies spy the uniform of France and forthwith their exit from this vale of tears would be short and not especially sweet.

In the rank alongside a cautious voice hailed him and he swung over to meet 'Arold's anxious glance.

" 'Ow about it, cockey? When do we break awye?"

"Sometime before dawn. We'd stand a fifty-fifty break if we could lay our hooks on some A-rab duds—" replied the sergeant while the night echoed with the noise of that unexpected skirmish. "It's plum sooicidal to desert in uniform."

"We'll 'ave to," was the cockney's gloomy verdict. "Gawd, did yer see the narsty glint in old Colonel Sowchay's heye? Blarst you, any'ow." The cockney spat viciously into the dust. "If you and yer disgustin' thirst 'adn't dragged me orf bounds—"

From his height, Lemuel regarded his companion with mingled pain and pity and his hand meditatively stroked his long jaw. "I may be cuckoo, Bud, but somehow I don't seem to remember issuing no G.O. ordering you to come along."

Before he could reply a sudden diapason roar made the bare hills reëcho and the starlight tinted 'Arold's wizened features a faint silver as he glanced quickly back towards the indistinct outlines of Agadés.

"Airplanes warmin' up! 'Ell must be bustin' loose when they rout out the swivel chair soljers."

"Yes, guess that means old Sowchay's been forced into a surprise attack—that's likely our only chance now that Ahmadu's crowd's agin us."

Louder grew the drone of airplane engines as Lemuel's little detachment quit the caravan track and struck out over the hard dry earth for a range of low hills that terminated the eastern horizon.

"About ready to take off," he remarked.

"Detachment, halt!" Lieutenant Aymard's voice sounded a little anxious as the column obeyed and stood peering uneasily at a stretch of sun-blasted earth where a number of smooth hillocks afforded cover for a would-be ambusher.

"As skirmishers—march!" Hardly had the last syllable fallen from Lieutenant Aymard's sun-cracked lips than certain of the Legionnaires trotted out to either flank, taking interval as they went.

"Stick close," Lemuel cautioned the cockney corporal. "Mebbe we'll get a good chance to vamoose sooner'n we think."

"Name of a little spotted blue baboon," growled Sergeant-major Pelletier. "Why deploy? Every lousy recruit knows that the Shereef has retreated to Yarda."

"Yarda? Wot's that?"

"Another of those garbage dump towns about five kilometers away. Reckon that's where those planes will be headin'—"

SULLENLY THE MARCHING Legionnaires stared upwards when the roar of airplane engines grew very loud indeed and Lemuel, peering into the purple sky, presently made out a squadron of four bombers flying so low that he could distinguish the red, white and blue cocards on their under wings.

'Arold heaved a gusty sigh of nervousness. " 'Ope they don't send arter us—'Ow soon do you think we'd better break awye?"

"Not yet. Wait until we get among more of them buttes. Work 'way out on the right flank. Get me? I'll be there, too. Then we'll just lose contact. Your water bottle full?"

The neck cloth on 'Arold's *képi* fluttered when he sharply inclined his head. "Yus, but I ain't got nothink to eat save that 'og fodder called emergency rations."

"Too bad," said the American sergeant stonily. "It's all I got, too.

"Slow 'em down, Anderson," he warned a bandy legged Norwegian corporal, "we're runnin' ahead o' our center."

Strung out in front of the main body was a shadowy line of skirmishers, each man some twenty yards from the next. Warily they picked their way along, their enormous packs making them look like queer hunchbacks. Now a Legionnaire would momentarily disappear from sight, now another, for the broken ground had been reached.

Behind the skirmishers, squad columns of eight Legionnaires marched, ready to support any threatened point. Back of all these was an indistinct black mass which marked the main body.

Very bitter were Lemuel's thoughts as, pistol in hand, he moved further and further out on the right flank. Damn the luck all the way to hell and back. Wouldn't something like this happen just when a commission was in reach? Yep, at the end of this campaign he'd have had a brevet lieutenancy if Obregon hadn't been there in the inn and if that cutthroat Ahmadu hadn't tripped over the flight sergeant's foot.

Obregon again! That guy sure was poison!

As the country became rougher and the skirmishers more occupied with picking their routes, the long limbed sergeant became increasingly wary. 'Arold's stubby figure, too, was drifting away from the long line of black figures.

"There's the place," he muttered when he beheld an especially rugged hillock looming into sight not far off to the right. There was another one beyond that.

Good, they'd make their break in a minute now. He drew a deep breath. His eyes ever probing the *driss* thickets which sprouted forlornly all about, he commenced to skirt the base of the hillock.

Cautiously, unostentatiously the cockney corporal started after him when the other skirmishers became lost to sight on the left of the mound. Three strides more, and the would-be deserters were hidden from the rest of the detachment.

"Beat it for the next hill," Lemuel called in an undertone. "There's some bushes there—"

Both Legionnaires began to run at top speed over the cement-hard ground towards a little gully that would afford shelter—but suddenly Lemuel's long form halted dead in its tracks, then whirled about.

"Jeeze to Jenny! Quick!" As he turned his left hand flew to his N.C.O.'s whistle, his right to the holstered pistol at his side.

He lost no time, for the very excellent reason that the gully was jammed with a dark mass of men and animals— and the men wore veils over their faces.

One short blast his whistle screamed then, to the pained astonishment of the skirmishers, a black wave seemed to rise over that long, crescent shaped hill perhaps two hundred yards away. At once wild howls of *"Lah-il-lah-il-Allah!"* shattered the night stillness and the wave poured down over the near slope.

3

THE LEGION FIGHTS

WITH EVEN MORE speed than they had quitted their detachment, the would-be deserters dashed back towards their comrades—and Colonel Souchet's firing squad—amid a volley of bullets that moaned all about them and struck the ground with vicious *phwits!*

A bugle blared "recall," whereat the rest of the skirmishers began to run like mad to rejoin the main body which Lieutenant Aymard was calmly forming in a flat ellipse.

From the horde of onrushing Touaregs burst a crackle of rifle reports mingled with the deeper booming roar of ancient, but stout, *moukhalas,* or muzzle loading muskets.

Among the Legion ranks things happened very promptly and precisely. In less than a minute from the moment Lemuel had stumbled upon that little enemy flanking party, the detachment had assembled into a compact double rank. Lieutenant Aymard, his eyeglasses gleaming dully, strode back and forth, superbly calm and efficient now that the issue was joined.

"*Bon, mes enfants,* use magazine fire when the whistles blow."

"And shoot straight, you clubfooted gorillas," added Sergeant Frost with deep feeling.

"If you miss, sacred specimens of tripe, you will never live to miss again," warned the worthy Pelletier, jerking out his automatic.

Very still was the detachment, but the *"Ul-ul-ul-ullah Akbar!"* of the Touaregs made enough noise for both sides. On either flank stood a sergeant, pistol levelled and with spare clips ready in his left hand. Sergeant Frost on the right and Sergeant-major Pelletier on the left.

"Ready!" cried the lieutenant.

"Ready!" echoed the sergeants.

Tighter grew the lines about the American's mouth as the charge gathered momentum.

"Aim!" "Aim!" "Aim!"

Lemuel glanced down along the front rank. They were kneeling now and sighting steadily at the Touareg mass of horse and camel men; above them stood the second rank.

"Lah! Lah!" shrieked the Touaregs and, standing high in their stirrups, brandished needle pointed iron lances which veterans among the Legionnaires feared far more than the heterogeneous firearms of this unexpected *harka.*

"They're easy two hundred o' them soap dodgers," yelled Lemuel, fully aware that there were at least twice that many attackers. "Steady, boys, aim at their horses."

"Four hundred—don't lie," called a giant Serb. "Would you cheat us of our glory?"

As is often the case, a macabre sort of humor rippled down the rank of waiting Legionnaires. One hundred against four hundred, odds long enough to take the breath of any soldier; yet with incomparable steadiness the blue and white ranks watched the howling avalanche of death sweep headlong down upon them.

LEMUEL FIXED HIS steady gray eyes on Lieutenant Aymard's sword hand. When that blade flashed down he would blow his whistle and then—well, those who lived would see what happened.

The drumming of hoofs grew louder like the throb of kettle drums, as the fleeter horsemen commenced to outstrip their camel mounted comrades who, higher and more distinctly seen on the light-colored Meharis, presented admirable targets.

"Horsemen first!" Lemuel called out, eyes still fixed on the elusive glimmer of the lieutenant's sword blade.

Bullets commenced to sigh and whine through the air and Dimitropous, a Greek Legionnaire, cried out and sank forward on his face.

Suddenly, the bright blade wavered. Ah, it sank! *Phiw-e-e-e* Lemuel's whistle screamed, to be instantly drowned out in a thunderous, crashing report.

Hills, ground, and a maddened charger, galloping far in advance of the rest, were briefly illumined. Darkness again!

Click-clock! went the rifle mechanisms. *Crash! Click-clock! Crash!*

The Legion fire was as regular as the stroke of a well-oiled engine and as deadly as the breath of Siva the Destroyer.

Sergeant Frost, firing at such horsemen as rode out on the flank of the Touareg force, caught the horrible screams of wounded horses, the shriek of wounded men and the bubbling groans of crippled camels.

Click-clock! Like a metallic sentence of death was the snap of the ejectors.

Less than fifty yards in front of the kneeling rank there

materialized, with magic suddenness, a terrible, kicking mound of fallen men and animals.

Crash! The fourth volley mowed down the Touaregs further back and suddenly the survivors—two hundred strong at least—veered off to the left and right and galloped away at top speed.

At this point was displayed some very pretty snap-shooting, in which the yelling Legionnaires emptied one high peaked saddle after another.

"Will they come back?" panted a wild-eyed Dutch recruit.

"Sure," Lemuel grunted as he crammed a fresh clip into his automatic, "but not for a while. That's them ornery Touaregs all over. Them cheap Johns stake everything on a charge and if it don't make a ten strike right off, they beat it. If the rest o' them *mal hombres* had kept on comin', most of us woulda been cat meat by now."

"I do not understand it," Lieutenant Aymard remarked with profane embellishments. "These *misérables* are Touareg of a type we have not met before—their veils are blue and not black or white."

There followed an unpleasant but necessary interval in which the wounded Touaregs, fighting like the human tigers they were, were dispatched to those joys reserved for such followers of Mohammed as die fighting the accursed Infidel.

WHEN THE LAST Touareg was draining out his life on the hard gray earth, all the horses and camels that were not hopelessly crippled were immediately collected and sent off to the rear with a brief report of the skirmish.

"Kinda quiet all of a sudden," Lemuel remarked when

he got up from arranging a bandage on a Legionnaire's shattered leg. "Wonder how we stand?"

Apparently the first engagement over to the right had also come to an end, for deep silence reigned over the desert. The dead of both sides were allowed to remain exactly where they fell; arms and equipment untouched, since it was far more imperative to dig in on that hill which commanded the pass of El Yarda.

"Fat chance we 'ave of gettin' awye now," 'Arold murmured when opportunity came for the exchange of a few words. "The 'ole country's alive wiv Touaregs."

"Yep, reckon our chance is gone," Lemuel admitted. "It would be sure death to high-tail for the tall timber. 'Pears like all we can do is to sit tight and hope—Hello, here come the planes again—Guess they laid their eggs while we was busy just now—"

Overhead droned the planes—black ungainly shapes momentarily blotting out bright patterns of stars.

"One arm-chair hero has been shot down, it would seem," Sergeant-major Pelletier suddenly remarked. "There are only three—before there were four. But, *nom du diable!* What is this?"

"Halt! *Qui vive?*"

From the half darkness at the foot of the ridge came the ringing challenge of an outpost.

Arms hastily snatched up were laid down again when four Legionnaires from the Seventh, headed by a gaunt captain, came up the hill at the double.

Sergeant Frost stiffened where he stood superintending the excavation of the rifle pits. So it had come already!

'Arold, with that calm philosophy of the mentally unimaginative, shrugged and put down his entrenching tool.

"The gyme's up, Lem."

"Shut up, you blasted fathead!" hissed Lemuel in a swift undertone. "Let's listen—maybe it's something else."

Fixedly, the anxious sergeant's eyes studied the outlines of Lieutenant Aymard's straight, soldierly form as he stood to salute. The bearded captain returned it and hurried forward.

"Glad you're safe, Aymard," he panted as he scanned the fox holes which were commencing to dot both sides of the pass. "The devil himself is to pay—that condemned rascal Ahmadu's *harka* has already fallen upon our flank. The whole column is in the gravest of danger."

"Already?" The word burst from Aymard's lips. "Impossible! Ahmadu's men could not learn so soon—There must be a mistake! Captain Sedoux—there must!"

Vigorously, the bearded captain nodded. "A mistake, yes—*'cré nom de sort,* yes!"

"But—I do not understand—" persisted Aymard. "How could—"

"Never mind that now, lieutenant."

Then came the words Lemuel had long dreaded to hear.

"Colonel Souchet wishes to know if there is in your detachment a sergeant, an American, who is called Frost?"

So the fat was in the fire! The American's flat stomach felt strangely empty. Damn Obregon, anyhow!

"YES, LE SERGEANT FROST is with me—A troublesome rascal but a soldier of the best—What do you wish with him?"

"That he will later learn," snapped Captain Sedoux. "Send for him at once."

"*Ohé*, Frost—report here!"

"Stay where you are, Bud," Lemuel whispered as he climbed out of the foxhole. "I got you into this."

"Like 'ell I will,'"Arold objected and brushed the white dust from his uniform with short nervous slaps. "I was in it as much as you was."

His face more like that of a Sioux brave than ever, Lemuel strode over to the waiting group.

"*Mon lieutenant?*"

"This is the man," Lieutenant Aymard said and his eyes behind their bright lenses looked very troubled. "I hope that—"

"*Bien.*" The bearded captain's gaze came to rest on Lemuel as he and 'Arold snapped a precise salute. "Sergeant Frost—Colonel Souchet has heard things concerning you."

"Yes, *mon capitaine.*" His gaunt features were immobile, but Lemuel's brain seemed on fire. What a triple damned fool he'd been to go off bounds with a commission almost in reach—but—well, he'd never been anything but a fool—

"Sir," his bearded features very grave, Captain Sedoux turned stiffly on Lieutenant Aymard who had already begun to protest, "under special orders of the officer commanding, Sergeant Frost is relieved from further duty with the Third Platoon and I am directed to take charge of him and his *copain.*"

"Yes, *mon capitaine.*" Lieutenant Aymard sighed regretfully.

Sick at heart, the big sergeant was aware that the other

N.C.O.'s and the privates were staring like schoolboys at a hoochy-koochy dance.

Numbly, Lemuel's fingers undid the flap of his pistol holster, but apparently Captain Sedoux considered the four alert Legionnaires at his back an ample insurance against trouble, for he said nothing.

"Come with me and bring that *demi-litre* of a corporal with you. He is your *copain*, is he not?"

"Yus, sir," growled 'Arold sturdily. "I'm 'is pal and I'm in it same as 'e is."

"You always was a fool," Lemuel reproached, as they turned to follow Captain Sedoux down the slope.

In silence the four Legionnaires of the guard fell in behind the culprits, their heavy rhythmic tread sounding like a dead march in Lemuel's ear.

"Not a bloomin' earthly chance for us now," whispered 'Arold. "Wish to 'ell them Touaregs 'ad 'eld off till we was clear."

But the sergeant, towering above him, made no reply. Lemuel was wondering what lay ahead. Of course he'd lie himself black in the face to save 'Arold. Good, cantankerous, loyal 'Arold. No wonder the English had conquered half the world. Though born and bred in the gutter, the little cockney corporal now, more than ever, showed the innate sturdiness of his race.

WHEN THEY HAD passed among the stiff and neglected dead of the skirmish, and the detachment position was lost to sight, the bearded captain halted and whirled about. Behind the two N.C.O.'s, the Legionnaires halted also, their eyes alone successfully piercing the gloom.

"Now it's come," Lemuel decided. "Going to slip us the works on the quiet, so's it won't hurt the morale none."

"Sergeant," the captain's features, lean and sharp as those of a greyhound, loomed very close, "Colonel Souchet has frequently told me he considers you the most resourceful, experienced, intelligent and troublesome N.C.O. in the Sixth Company—Believing you to be a good tracker, liar, and—what you call it—bluffer, he has selected you for a mission—A mission which means victory, or disaster and terrible death for every man of the column."

"Ulp!" said Lemuel deep in his throat. What was this *hombre* saying?

"Gawd!" choked 'Arold. " 'E ain't twigged yet!"

The eyes of both Legionnaires peered, bright and incredulous, from beneath their heat-warped *képi* brims. Was this all a trick? But no—no attempt had been made to arrest them. Instantly Lemuel's agile brain read the situation aright.

Evidently the worthy colonel was yet in blissful ignorance.

He cast a somber eye at an eagle featured Armenian Legionnaire who, momentarily disappearing behind a huge pile of rocks, reappeared with a large bundle under his arm.

"Now, sergeant, and you, too, corporal, give closely of your attention," Captain Sedoux directed. "It is Colonel Souchet's wish that you at once disguise yourselves and thus penetrate into the town of Yarda—It lies perhaps six kilometers beyond the pass you were guarding—Not an easy matter, of a certainty not. That is why he chose you."

"Get into Yarda!" grunted Lemuel. "But, *mon capitaine,*

the Shereef's headquarters are supposed to be there—or were."

"Precisely." The bearded captain's teeth glimmered briefly in the starlight. "That is what *Monsieur le Colonel* must find out before ten of the morning. You are of the same tall build as the Touareg themselves and carry yourself as one. Above all you are quick witted—or thought to be—It is to be hoped that you are, for to be suspected in Yarda, is to die—well, very unpleasantly."

"And the town's just been bombed," remarked Lemuel. A swell assignment! It was hard to sound unenthusiastic, for a great and cheering light had broken over his agile mind. He foresaw several interesting possibilities to the situation. Good-by firing squad! With Touareg dress, fast horses and a head start—well, if he and 'Arold couldn't make the Nigerian border in about two days they deserved to be shot. What a break!

"Now understand well, sergeant," Captain Sedoux was saying, "this is not an order. *Monsieur le Colonel* does not order men to take such—er, grave risks."

"How about it, Bud?" Very long and serious was Sergeant Frost's craggy face.

'Arold shrugged elaborately. "We'll most likely get scragged in Yarda, but anythink is better than—"

"Sure, we'll do it, sir." Lemuel dealt his friend a warning kick on the shins. "Ain't guaranteeing results, though. How about the corporal, sir? He don't look like no Touareg I ever see—why, he ain't knee high to a burro."

"He can be a Fula slave," the captain decided briefly. "Many of them are short. You will be in Yarda only a short time—I hope."

"But how about the palaver? What if somebody asks questions?"

"We will put a bandage atout your jaw—you are wounded and cannot talk; and *le corporal* can be a tongueless slave—there are many such among the Touaregs."

FIFTEEN MINUTES LATER it would have taken an expert to recognize either of the badly wanted N.C.O. Legionnaires. Garbed in the flowing regalia of a Touareg who had been shot through the head during the recent skirmish, the American's lean and supple figure did bear a striking resemblance to those fierce overlords of the Sahara. Beneath the black *litham* one of the Legionnaires tied a dingy rag bandage and as only Lemuel's eyes and nose were visible, the effect was strikingly realistic. Frost's hopes became almost radiantly bright and he fought to suppress a burst of laughter. Lord, *wouldn't* old Souchet rave!

'Arold, similarly clad but with a white face cloth which was the distinguishing mark of the *billah*, or Touareg slave, strutted ludicrously back and forth. "Feel like orl the Seven Barrison Sisters at once," he remarked. "Buss me, Lem."

"*Voilà*, sergeant." With his own hands Captain Sedoux buckled to Lemuel's broad leather belt a four foot sword which had been very recently the property of a Hoggar Touareg.

"And now, my braves," said the worthy captain, "here come the horses you are to ride, so I will explain the importance of your mission." His words became charged with the utmost gravity. "Do not for an instant forget that five hundred lives depend on the information you bring back. *And you must get back!*"

Very penetrating was the glare he fixed on Lemuel.

"Three forces are against us now; Ayoub, his reënforcements under Caïd Haroun, and, thanks to those accursed
Legionnaires, Ahmadu's clan. Some twelve thousand men
in all."

"Seems hardly enough," murmured Lemuel softly.

"Our only hope is to defeat these forces in detail—
before they can unite. If the Shereef is still in Yarda, we
attack there. If he has left the town, we pass to the south
towards el Kebab and hope to take this troublesome clog in
the flank, destroying him before his reënforcements under
Caïd Haroun arrive."

"I see," the American nodded slowly. "After licking
Haroun's crowd, it will be easy to swing south and cripple
Ahmadu's lootenants—"

"Precisely, but if we learn nothing of the Shereef's intent,
we must in any case move by ten o'clock or die at the hands
of the united force. Failing your information, the column
will pass to the south to destroy Haroun, leaving the thrice
accursed Ayoub free on the flank. You understand, do you
not, sergeant?"

"Yes, sir."

"Remember, now, you have only to penetrate the town,
look about, and see whether the Touaregs are in Yarda, if
they have gone, or if they plan to go. Learn, moreover, if
Ayoub is fortifying the town, and whether, God forbid, the
forces of Caïd Haroun have already joined him."

"Yes, sir." Lemuel's broad right hand flashed up to his
turban in salute, and Sedoux frowned.

"*Mon Dieu!* what a fist! You must keep that tattooed
paw out of sight, for the Touaregs' hands are small and do

not have mermaids on them. Keep them hidden in your sleeves."

"Yes, sir."

The bearded captain held out his hand. "*Alors adieu, mes enfants.* You have only to be cautious, follow this caravan track and, above all, get back before dawn."

With the ease of an ex-member of the 4th U.S. Cavalry, Lemuel swung up into the high pommeled Arab saddle on the back of a nervous, cream-colored barb, and 'Arold, ex-trooper of His Britannic Majesty's 9th Hussars, mounted his horse with no greater effort.

"Good-by, sir."

Touching heels to his spirited mount, Lemuel shifted the long Touareg lance to his right hand and, with 'Arold close behind, cantered off down the winding track ahead while the cold desert wind whipped their sour smelling robes about them.

4

LUCK?

"GAWD!" CHUCKLED 'AROLD when Sergeant Frost reined in among the concealing shadows of a deep *wadi*. "Wot a bit o' luck! 'Ere I was thinkin' 'ow Captain Sedoo and Co. was going to drag us orf to chokey, and instead wot does 'e do but give us 'orses and disguise!"

"Sure," grunted Lemuel, thoughtfully scanning the shadowy desert, "that was a one dyed-in-the-wool break. But—"

"But?—Wot you talking about?" 'Arold's eyes, seen through the gap of his white face veil, were both suspicious and uneasy. "You ain't barmy enough to think o' goin' into that ruddy death trap called Yarda?"

"I was thinking of it," the bigger horseman admitted gruffly.

"Garn!" 'Arold urged his barb up alongside of Lemuel's. "Don'cher twig wot the colonel's doing?"

"No."

" 'Ell!" The cockney's voice was charged with scorn. "Ain't you the thick headed numskull!"

"Shut up, you ornery half pint, or I'll nacherally jest spit on you and drown you."

Momentarily failed by words, the cockney corporal tried

to spit, quite forgetting that his newly acquired face veil intervened. Then he said, "Wye, it's plain as the nose on yer ugly fyce. Of course, Colonel Souchet 'as learned 'oo it was as did in Ahmadu and, because military executions is bad for the morale, 'e's gettin' rid o' us this wye. Oh, 'e's a cute one, 'e is!

"Come on, Lem, we'd better leg it for the Ivory Coast before one of them Touareg *'arkas* catch us and cuts us to 'amburgers. Wot d' yer sye?"

He peered eagerly up at that long, black veiled figure which rode with turbaned head pensively bowed.

"Mebbe, Bud, mebbe." Over the dull *clip! clop!* of the hoofs the big sergeant's voice sounded preoccupied.

For all of five minutes the two rode silently along the caravan track which had been old when Rome was being sacked by the Gothic hordes of Alaric. Then, with the manner of a man who has arrived at a difficult decision, Lemuel lifted his head, grotesque in a compact turban that was bound with twin rings of black horsehair.

"Bud," he said, "I figger mebbe you're right, but just the same I don't reckon Colonel Souchet is the kind of *hombre* who'd hand us over to the Touaregs. Sorry I am to say it, but it 'pears to me like he's puttin' a heap of confidence on us two, which makes it mighty hard to let him down. You heard what Captain Sedoo said about us being good and resourceful scouts?"

"It's you 'e means, not me," objected 'Arold with characteristic frankness. "You're the one wot cooks up all the deviltry. And the wye o' gettin' out o' it." His pinched features fell into a scowl. "But you ain't really barmy enough to think o' going into Yarda, are yer?"

"I'm forty kinds o' plain and fancy damned fools—but I—I reckon so," the ex-cavalryman admitted shamefacedly.

He fumbled in the leather pouch at his belt. "Here's the compass. Head south, southwest—I reckon you can find your way all right—"

Astonishment, deep and painful, was engraved in every line of 'Arold's shadowy features.

"Wot! Yer ain't goin' on?"

"I'm just a plain damn fool, I allow, but Lem Frost has yet to disobey a direct order." He held out the compass. "So long, Bud—good luck to you."

'Arold sighed and shrugged as he said, "Put the ruddy thing awye. Since ye're so smart, 'ow does yer figure we can get into Yarda?" The words faded on the cockney corporal's muffled lips, for off to the right sounded the dull clatter of dislodged stones rolling down a depression.

AS ONE, BOTH horsemen reined in and then swerved to the shelter of a huge pile of rocks. Powerful and quick as a puma, Lemuel promptly thrust his lance into the earth— point down—swung off his mount and clapped his broad hand over the barb's soft muzzle; then 'Arold expertly blindfolded both horses.

With bated breath they watched, emerging from the shadows of a *wadi,* a large body of horsemen which, if their dark cloaks and long lances meant anything, must be a band of Touaregs out on a reconnaissance or a maraud- ing expedition. Numbering some twenty or thirty, the Touaregs filed by in almost ghostly silence, and Lemuel's eyes narrowed to see that behind the camels of some of the riders there trotted certain wretches who, with hands tied behind them, did their best to keep up with the swift, swaying pace of the meharis.

When that swift little column had become lost in the darkness, Lemuel, suddenly struck by an inspiration, pressed his mouth to 'Arold's ear.

"Mount up quick! We'll ride well back o' them until we get near Yarda, then we'll close up. Mebbe we can get by the outposts that way."

And so it turned out. Long before the walls of Yarda—even more crumbled and ruinous than those of Agadés—came into view, other detachments of Touaregs appeared on the dimly lit desert. Evidently a concentration was in order, for by tens, fives and even singly, these fierce denizens of the lower Sahara—many of them splendidly accoutered—appeared, to lift rifle or spear in salute and to ride on into Yarda. Thus it was not wholly surprising that Lemuel and 'Arold rode unchallenged among the pungent camel dung fires of the scattered encampments dotting the plain outside of the town itself.

Apparently contemptuous of a French attack, the Touaregs had left wide open the town's ponderous gate and the two spies passed beneath it without drawing so much as a grunt from tribesmen drowsing among the shadows.

"This way," Lemuel muttered and turned his horse down a rubbish littered gap between the time-worn walls and the first row of blank faced, flat topped houses which, without exception, were equipped with strongly barred windows and powerful wooden doors.

Without easing their cinches, the adventurers dismounted and made their horses fast to a well gnawed rack, which, if one were to judge by the condition of the ground, had recently been used by many animals.

"How's your courage, Bud?" Lemuel inquired as he rested his iron lance against the wall.

"Not a bit dahn'earted—" came the cheerful reply. "But lemme larf now or I will later. Strike me pink, Lem, if yer don't look like a cross between a blinkin' bailey dancer and 'Amlet's ghost gone out for a constitootional."

Lemuel peered cautiously about with a smile twisting his wide slash of a mouth. Good old 'Arold, cracking jokes when he was scared stiff.

" 'Pears like there ain't much goin' on around here," he commented. "Reckon we'd better *andar* further into this foul scented burg."

GATHERING HIS DARK blue *djellaba* closer about him, he led off up an ancient stair, worn down by the passing of countless thousands of bare feet. Lord! how black it was up there. The houses, seemingly built one on top of another, also leaned towards each other, shutting out the feeble glow of the stars.

Hampered by the long, unfamiliar swords at their sides, the two N.C.O.'s continued to climb, their Touareg sandals scuffing softly on the greasy steps, until they came upon the blasted ruins of several houses that had very recently spilled their ruins into the street. Near by a shrill wailing made the walls reëcho.

"Air bomb," was Lemuel's brief whisper. "They must be hoppin' mad." He was finding the task assigned him harder than he had imagined, for at this late hour there was no accurate way of telling how many of the Touaregs were in the town. Behind each of these silent portals might be one, two, ten—or none of the enemy.

Now and again the spies encountered parties of burly Hausa Negroes, impressed for duty by their Touareg overlords since—fortunately—the numbers of the Forgotten of God are not in proportion to their fighting abilities. In the semi-darkness these huge mercenaries, with their scarred cheeks, their sharp-filed teeth and their bushy heads of hair, made awesome figures.

"Wot narsty lookin' shines!" was 'Arold's verdict. "Bet they go abaht frightening bad youngsters in their orf moments."

Further into the depths of the venerable town did Lemuel lead the way, keeping careful track of his progress until the atmosphere quite lost the clean, sweet smell of the desert to become tinctured with the stench of rancid offal, stale dung and sewage of a dozen kinds.

It was a ticklish business, tramping along those narrow, lightless passages where mangy scavenger dogs snarled and snapped at their skirts.

Suddenly the spies came face to face with a group of Touaregs who, tall and stately, appeared around a bend in an alley. One of them barred the passage, at the same time calling out something and Lemuel's blood pressure commenced to climb as, very convincingly, he uttered inarticulate noises and pointed to his bandaged jaw.

At once the Touareg stepped close and peered intently into the impostor's face.

5

TORTURE

IT WAS A ticklish moment, for the noisome alley was not quite three feet wide, and to pass each other, the two parties must flatten against opposite walls and brush by. Firmly, Lemuel pushed on, his nostrils filled with the rank body odor of men who had not been bathed since birth. Exhalations, foul as the reek of feet long unwashed, fanned Lemuel's face as the Forgotten of God pressed flat against the opposite wall and hitched their weapons aside.

After a nerve racking moment they were by, but Lemuel was disturbed to notice the leading Touareg still staring after him, suspicion written in his every limb. As the two spies started on, the other party called after them.

"Leg it!" Lemuel hissed and, turning quickly down the first passage to the right, darted into what proved to be a roofed over *soûk* where a detachment of long-limbed Touaregs lay snoring in doorways and beneath the empty stalls of the merchants.

"Eus beur! Stop! *Aoukerif!* Halt!"

But the fugitives only put on more speed when the dreaded cry of, "Spies! *Djouacis!*" arose.

Behind pattered the feet of pursuers and it was not until the fugitives had become inextricably lost amid a maze of winding black alleys in the heart of Yarda that they succeeded in shaking off the pursuit.

"Close, as the barber said," Lemuel panted when they halted in the gloom of the archway.

"Yus, the whole bloomin' town seems to be awyke. What a jolly little rat 'ole this is. We'd better pad the 'oof."

Hearts still thudding from the narrowness of their escape, the two studied the dim doorways about them, then 'Arold inquired:

"Wot does ya think? Is the Shereef's main body 'ere or ain't it?"

"Can't tell for sure yet," Lemuel replied, "and we better not make no mistake. Guess we'd better mosey; along over to the other side of town and see what's what, maybe."

They had just set off when from among a group of tall and shadowy buildings off to the left a fearful voice, rising in a crescendo of agony, set the hair to tingling on the nape of Lemuel's neck.

"Oh-h-h-h, o-h, God—" it wailed. "Kill me—kill me! Stop it—Oh-h! Why can't I die?"

Then followed such heart-rending screams of anguish as Lemuel had not previously heard in all his turbulent years of adventuring. In that awful outcry was the insensate scream of the wounded horse and the throbbing, throat-tearing wails of a creature driven mad by pain. Then, even more horrible, arose the shout of laughter—cold, jeering, mocking laughter.

In dismayed silence the spies regarded each other; *that voice had spoken in English!*

"SOME POOR DEVIL of a prisoner gettin' the works—"

growled Lemuel, his eyes narrowed to glittering cracks. "And they're sure makin' him sing."

"Yus." Beneath its dingy white turban 'Arold's head inclined. "Fair gives a bloke the 'orrors."

"Help! Help! They're killing me!"

"Obregon!" And beneath the heavy malodorous robes Lemuel stiffened as though a hot iron had touched the small of his back. He started forward, but 'Arold desperately clung to the taller man's arm.

"Drop it—we carn't go," he pleaded fiercely. "We carn't do nothink. That rotten mucker ain't no pal of yours."

"No—but he's a white man—"

Lemuel was shaking his powerful right arm, but the smaller Legionnaire clung to it with the desperate strength of a bull dog fastened to a bull's neck.

"Don't be a fool, Lem," 'Arold's voice rang out. "Carn't you see? That dirty Chilean's going to die. Now we can go back to the Legion."

Temptation, well-nigh overwhelming, battled in the big sergeant's soul—Common sense, everything advised against interference.

"Wot's that back-bitin garlic destroyer to yer?" the English corporal pursued eagerly. " 'E ain't done you nothink but 'arm. Let 'im die—then we're safe!"

It was as 'Arold said—they could return if Obregon died—but somehow that dreadful cry still lingered in his ears and, beneath the unfamiliar robes, Lem's wide shoulders straightened.

"I reckon you're right, Bud," said he, clipping off his words short, "but Obregon's a white man and too damn good a scrapper to be carved to kybobs by any bunch o'

He squirmed to get free as the bayonets drove at him.

mangy, soap dodging A-rabs. So long, Bud, see you by the horses."

So saying he easily wrenched off the distracted cockney's detaining hand and, stepping briskly along, set off down a malodorous passage towards those heart-chilling cries which were flung back and forth by the dingy walls above.

Desperately, Sergeant Frost was bribing his conscience with the hope that he might learn something of military importance over yonder. Moreover, he reminded himself, he certainly was not going to throw away his own life in a hopeless attempt to rescue the unhappy Chilean—all he planned was to speed a bullet to cut short the torture of the unhappy wretch.

Deep-set eyes ever on the alert, he dodged silently from one nail studded doorway to the next, broad right hand gripping the butt of that heavy .45 with which he was as deadly as the Olympian god with his thunderbolts.

He looked back and was a little conscience stricken to

behold the faithful 'Arold following a few yards behind, his stocky figure more distinctly revealed by the throbbing glare of fire reflected from the façade of a tall building above.

A moment later they swaggered boldly out into a broad street where armed Touaregs were continually coming and going with a soft scuffing of sandaled feet. A small group stood looking at another house which had been blown into grotesque and dusty shapelessness by an aërial bomb.

"No wonder they're giving the boy friend the works," Lemuel murmured. "Reckon most of the bombs lit on this side of the town. Damn' fool must have flown too low and got shot down."

The tortured Chilean's cries were growing louder and mingled with them were the screams of some new victim. **HEART THUDDING WILDLY** beneath his robes of heavy white wool, the gaunt sergeant boldly passed beneath a gateway to descry one of the most unforgettable tableaux he had ever beheld.

The square, hemmed in by firelit buildings, measured perhaps fifty by a hundred feet, and was packed to suffocation with hundreds of fierce, weapon-bristling figures. Staring in avid enjoyment, the lordly Touaregs were squatting on their hams, with a dense crowd of Fula, Hausa and Senegalese warrior-slaves at their backs.

Ever mindful of his purpose, Lemuel cast never a glance across the square, but, arrogantly as any real Touareg, forced a way through the edges of the crowd, heading towards an alley opening which was even narrower than the one he had just quitted. The crowd was thinner there and the alley mouth seemed a good place to shoot from.

"Range will be 'bout fifty yards," he silently estimated. "Poor old Obregon—"

When a cloud of wood smoke momentarily blinded the onlookers, he glanced back and was relieved to see the cockney corporal not three paces behind and vigorously shoving his way along.

Carefully Lem stepped over the legs of a gigantic tribesman who lay resting his weight on his elbows, staring at the fire with fierce, sombre eyes. Then a new smell struck Lemuel's nose—an odor something like that of an overdone steak—and a fresh yell of pain spurred his determination.

Arriving at the alley mouth he waited for 'Arold to come up. Then he whispered his plan.

"—Goin' to shoot Obregon—put him out of pain—See? We'll beat it soon's I shoot—tell me when—alley's clear."

"Right." Though his pale blue eyes glittered with excitement, the little cockney's voice was steady.

Breathing hard, Lemuel drew his pistol from its holster, threw off the safety catch and, perforce, studied that unforgettable scene being enacted beyond the leaping, licking fire.

Perhaps twelve feet above the court two heavy beams jutted from the side of a granary. From one of these dangled Flight Sergeant Obregon. The Chilean was as naked as the day he was born, his body shining yellow-red in the firelight from below, and his blackhead sank low on his hairy chest.

In a flash Lemuel saw that the Touaregs had lashed the prisoner's hands together behind his back, then by hoisting the unhappy aviator from the ground by his wrists had undoubtedly dislocated his shoulders and had left him to squirm and moan in ceaseless agony—feet barely clear of the ground.

But that which was drawing the attention of the crowd was a new spectacle. Swung head down from the other beam a howling native prisoner was being gradually lowered into the heart of the roaring fire. Frantically, the poor wretch's thin brown arms tried to beat aside the flames.

DELIBERATELY LEMUEL BRACED his long body against the wall and picked out just that portion of Obregon's chest he would aim at. He knew he would not miss—but the realization that he would in a moment now throw his life in the scales was a sobering thought.

"Go a'ead," came 'Arold's cautious voice—"orl clear be'ind."

Swiftly Lemuel's hand swept upwards, the .45 engulfed in its sinewy depths, but, just as he pressed the trigger, Fortune turned away her face. A Fula slave stepping hastily into the alley mouth stopped the grim faced sergeant's bullet with his kinky head.

Uttering a deep grunt, the slave spun half about before he toppled over and fell kicking like a shot rabbit.

Aware that the passing of each fraction of a second lessened their chances of escape, Lemuel whirled and was aghast to see a door opening beyond 'Arold. He leaped down the alley, but a small avalanche of yelling, white-clad figures effectively barred retreat down the passage.

Hash for breakfast! he told himself grimly and over 'Arold's shoulder dropped a yelling Touareg who had whipped out his sword and stood barring the alleyway.

Only subconsciously did the desperate Legionnaire hear
the sword clatter to the dirty stones, his whole intent being
to rescue 'Arold, who was locked in a desperate struggle
with a black slave twice his size.

"Keep on," he panted and shot the next man beyond
in a frantic effort to break through. Yells and shots rang
out from behind and in the powder filled alley everything
became kaleidoscopic. Black, brown and light tan faces
barring his way were momentarily lit by the flash of his
pistol. Ah, 'Arold had succeeded in killing the Negro with
a vicious upward thrust of his Touareg dagger.

No use. A furious torrent of Touaregs was closing in
from the direction of the courtyard. Hot greasy hands
clawed at his wrist and his last bullet only made a clean
white spot on the dingy wall of the house alongside. 'Arold
was already down.

"Hi yah-yah!"

Lemuel was insanely yelling a weird Comanche war cry
and flailing about with his clubbed pistol when the butt
of a *moukhala* crashed down on his head and a cascade of
fiery sparks fell before his eyes, completely shutting out
consciousness.

6

LEMUEL IS TESTED

THE SMELL OF wood smoke and of hot iron was strong in the nose of Sergeant Lemuel Frost when he once more became aware that this world can be a very wretched place. In swift succession came a number of exceedingly discouraging realizations. First, that his hands were securely lashed behind him with cruel efficiency; second, that his ankles as well were secured; and last that he lay with bruised face pressed to a very cold and dirty stone surface.

Next he realized that someone was dealing him a series of shattering kicks in the ribs by way of a restorative. Promptly, the prostrate sergeant decided that shamming unconsciousness would be no advantage. Accordingly he groaned, spat out a mouthful of blood and raised his head an inch or two. A movement which evoked a growl of delight from that ominous multitude which was but faintly revealed by the fire he had previously watched from a distance.

"Ha! the *Roumi* dog awakes."

A leather cased foot none too gently shoved his throbbing head sidewise and he found himself looking dazedly up at a figure which, from his position on the ground, seemed to be of colossal proportions.

"*Kelb ibn kelb!*" The veiled man above lifted his veil and spat full into Lemuel's face.

This individual, like the rest, wore a *litham,* but the doomed sergeant recognized the gold mounted dagger of a *Hadji* at his belt.

"Stand up, thou dog!" A Senegalese slave, undoubtedly a deserter from some French Colonial battalion, translated for Lemuel's benefit. So with the help of a few kicks, the sergeant arose dizzily.

Yes, no doubt that the worst had happened. Not twenty feet away lay 'Arold, bound, stripped of his native regalia and staring with sullen, bloodshot eyes up at the distant stars. The cockney seemed quite resigned, with that blessed hopelessness of the unimaginative, though the charred body of the tortured native lay to one side and Obregon still dangled from the beam, his semiconscious moaning audible in every lull.

"Since fightin' won't get us nowhere," Lemuel told himself, "I reckon it's a case of 'brains, do your stuff!'"

He tried to master his quivering nerves, but the flesh on his back crept when he beheld a half naked Hausa thrusting a pair of huge iron pincers into the fire.

Speaking through the Senegalese deserter, the Touareg chieftain haughtily commanded the prisoner to be brought near after Lemuel's ankle cords had been removed.

"Listen well, O despoiler of the dead and defiler of the salt," growled the Hausa, his filed teeth giving his ugly, flat visage a dog-like look, "and answer the questions of Ayoub, beloved of Fatima and Shereef of all the Touaregs."

So, mused Lemuel, as he had half expected, the man with the gold dagger and straight gray eyebrows was that redoubtable bandit whose slave raids into Dahomey and the Côte d'Ivoire had prompted this expedition which now seemed doomed to end in as overwhelming disaster as had ever befallen the Legion.

A SMILE TWISTED Lemuel's unshaven and battered features. "Hail, O mighty Shereef," he cried in execrable but quite understandable French. "Is this the way the Touaregs treat those who wish them well?" The gaunt American actually managed to look indignant.

Ayoub, when the interpreter had delivered this conversation, seemed highly amused and his powerful shoulders shook with a macabre merriment.

"Ho! Ho! Ho! Verily this is a madman among us— Whoever heard of a *Franzwazi* friend of the Targui?"

"Aye—O, Shereef—good friends, moreover."

This time Ayoub's principal vassals heard him and a general shout of grim laughter reëchoed in the courtyard.

'Arold abruptly deserted his steady inspection of the stars; and even the wretched Obregon, swinging like a sculptured image from the palm fiber rope, raised his heavy head a few inches.

"By the head of Shaitan!" chuckled the veiled chieftain as he tugged at a forked gray beard that protruded from below his *litham*. "Art thou mad?"

"No," replied Lemuel, desperately cool, "but I'm going to get mad pretty soon." He nodded to the Hausa guard. "Tell this blasted slave to cut loose my hands."

Mentally he cursed the Shereef's veil for concealing the reaction to his remarks.

Contemptuously ignoring the request, Ayoub said, "Art thou a brave man, O dog of a *Franzwazi?*"

"Most times," admitted the American modestly. "But I've been a coward just often enough to stay alive."

"That is fortunate." One of the Shereef's small, well modeled hands beckoned those slaves who had been heating the pincers.

Thick, purple-blue lips parted in ferocious grins, the Senegalese executioners stepped up and Lemuel became subconsciously aware that the rows of tribal scars on their foreheads were bright with sweat from the heat of the fire. In the huge paws of one of the slaves the pincers glowed a pale, scorching pink.

Sweat also broke out on Lemuel's brow. He would have to talk fast now. What terrible fear there was written on 'Arold's twitching features.

"This *Roumi* dog talks too much—Tear out his tongue!" commanded the stately figure in blue and white robes.

Instantly Lemuel was pinioned by half a dozen enormous slaves and his skin crept at the contact of those hot moist hands.

"Better not," yelled the desperate American and forced a smile to lips that were twitching with dread. "You'll lose a valuable ally."

Ayoub sharply turned his aquiline head. "Ally? Does the lion ally himself with the jackal?"

"Listen well, Shereef—early to-night the little man and I did you the biggest favor any European has ever done."

In the slit of the blue *litham* the Touareg's glittering black eyes paused, then shifted uncertainly. Perhaps the American's unflinching attitude had earned a modicum of consideration. Ayoub paused, raised his hand—not that this delay would in any way lessen the torments in store.

"What good hast thou done me, O son of a mangy she-camel?"

Every word must do its part, so to gain time Lemuel pretended to cough in a gust of wood smoke that was whirled up by the chill desert wind.

RINGED AROUND BY the Touaregs whose weapons continually glinted in the firelight, he made a dramatic figure when the fire flared suddenly to reveal the powerful muscles of his torso and the lavish tattooing on his arms.

"The great Shereef does not believe me, I see—" the hollow-eyed sergeant remarked.

"I do not!"

"Well, to prove that my words are true I ask you to order that *soldado*—" he nodded his disheveled head in Obregon's direction—"taken down. When he has recovered a little ask him who killed your enemy—Tchek Ahmadu."

"Ahmadu? *W'Allah!*" Ayoub started, then stepped forward, eyes narrowed in menace.

"If thou liest, accursed *Franzwazi*, rest assured thou shalt be three days in dying."

"So may it be if I lie." Splendid was Lemuel's sangfroid and 'Arold licked lips that had gone dry.

Commands crackled from Ayoub's lips and very shortly Obregon, groaning terribly, was lowered to the earth, untied and restored to consciousness by such crude means as the application of a red-hot iron to the small of his back.

"Oh, God! Kill me—noble—Shereef! I—I can stand no more," the Chilean whimpered.

"If this be a trick, accursed *Roumi*," snarled Ayoub—he seemed only afraid that the intelligence might be false, "thou shalt die a thousand deaths!"

"It is no trick," replied Lemuel calmly. "As you know, I have spoken no word to your prisoner, the man who lies yonder—"

From the tail of his eye he could see Obregon's utterly incredulous expression, could see sudden hope born on his swarthy features and witnessed the equally sudden death of those hopes. Two slaves abruptly hauled the pitiful wretch to his feet and dragged him forward, empurpled shoulders still distorted by dislocation.

"Speak!" With the butt of his camel whip, Ayoub brutally slashed the swaying Chilean across the face, so that the aviator's body jerked spasmodically. "Did the Tchek called Ahmadu die to-night?"

"Yes." Obregon's handsome head sagged in a feeble nod when the interpreter put the question.

"How did he die?" The Touareg's hawklike profile was not a foot from the Chilean's bloodied features.

"Mercy—" babbled the prisoner, quite misunderstanding the purpose of the question. "He—he was slain. I—I did not do it—it was—"

"Who slew him?" thundered the Shereef.

"I—I—don't—please. Why—two Legionnaires caused it—that man and the other—" His bloodshot eyes wavered to Lemuel's, but that astute individual was wholly occupied in studying what he could see of the Shereef's thin face.

"Then it *was* this *gaour* who slew that son and father of traitors. Why?"

"May it please the mighty Shereef," lied Lemuel with convincing glibness, "my friend and I are not Frenchmen—we were forced to fight for them. We hate them. We slew Ahmadu that you might profit by trouble between his followers and the accursed French. They have already fought—because of this we fled to your protection—There is much more we can tell you—"

"To trap us, no doubt—" Then, quite ignoring his prisoners, the Shereef spun about and, addressing his lieutenants, commenced a long harangue in Mahgreb.

THEN IT WAS that Lemuel would have gladly given his right hand for an inkling of what was being said, for the scales of Fate were very nicely adjusted now and a feather's weight would incline them towards life or death. Several times he caught the word "Ahmadu." What was being said? Could he get away and warn the anxious column waiting outside of Agadés?

Back to his burning brain flashed phrases of Captain Sedoux's explanation of the situation. "We must strike before any of these three forces become united—Failing information, we will attack Caïd Haroun." Lemuel decided to risk all in a bold assumption of the initiative.

"Listen to me, O Shereef of the dreaded Touaregs—time departs never to return—"

"Silence!" growled a bony one-eyed chieftain while drawing his robes back lest the fire catch them. "Why didst thou shoot thy pistol and slay the slave?"

"The dog I shot would have robbed us," Lemuel replied glibly. "The others I shot lest they slay me."

Shereef Ayoub, though sensing rare possibilities to the situation, appeared not to know what to make of this amazingly calm individual who, with torture irons not four feet away, acted as though he were commanding a *harka*.

"I promise nothing," he rasped, "but it now appears that thou hast not lied concerning Ahmadu—may the black dogs of Jehannum tear his entrails!—and I believe also that thou hast willingly quit the *harka* of the *Franzwazi.*"

Apparently the worthy Shereef was beginning to appreciate that the presence of a man who was familiar with French military formations and strategy could be made decidedly useful.

"Hakim!" He beckoned forward a man who was not a Touareg, but an Arab out of Egypt. "Straighten the shoulders of that accursed *Roumi* dog; then give him some clothes and bid him and these other *gaours* ponder upon the greatness of Allah and the wrath of Ayoub Behar."

Obregon now presented a truly miserable appearance. His unshaven features were bruised and stained with dirt and furrowed by tears of agony, while his tormented nervous system caused sudden twitchings and involuntary jerkings of his body.

"Merciful God—why didn't you let them kill me—" he whimpered and flinched when a guard passed near him.

"Well, Obregon," began Lemuel in English, " 'pears like I won't never get a chance to give you that licking I been keepin' for you."

"Ah, shut yer blasted 'ead, Lem," suddenly snarled 'Arold, gold teeth revealed in his furious expression. "We'd 'ave been safe out of Yarda by now if you 'adn't tried to play the big 'earted 'ero!"

LEMUEL, HOWEVER, WAS deep in thought, furiously assailing the problem of retrieving some particles of success out of this shattering disaster. Somewhere lay the answer. He was suddenly aware of the Chilean's incredulous stare.

"You," he demanded in a thin, reedy voice, "you risked your life for *me?*"

"Sure," grunted Lemuel dispassionately. "I'd save a yaller pup pain if I could."

The realization could not for a moment penetrate the flight sergeant's numbed brain.

"*Señor Dios*—I—I saw what happened to Tchek Ahmadu at the inn," he groaned, "and—and to think I was going to turn you in—What a vile swine I am—Since we are both to die very soon—I—I ask you to forgive—"

The ring of truth and earnestness was in the Chilean's voice and he feebly tried to hold out his right hand, but the pain of his tortured shoulders made him moan and abandon the effort.

"O.K.," the Indian featured sergeant nodded solemnly. "Bygones are bygones. Now, lemme try to figger how to get outta this here mess."

"Yer better 'ad," snarled the un-reconciled 'Arold. "You and yer yoomane instinks." He turned his grim little face on Obregon. "I don't trust yer, cully, not a bit, so I'll arsk yer to pass yer word never to say nothink about that row at the Three Moons—if we ever get back to the Legion."

A black scowl decked Obregon's sweaty forehead. "*Dios de Dios!* You rotten cockney rat! D'you think I'd be such a swine as to do that after what Frost risked for me?"

" 'Tain't impossible," returned 'Arold bitterly.

Whereupon the Chilean waxed eloquent and tears of earnestness were in his eyes as he vowed a silence deeper than that of the well known grave.

"Well, boys," Lemuel said a little later when the Touareg council appeared on the point of breaking up, "I got a play figgered out—but it's gotta be played close to the vest. Now get a load o' this. I'm going to advise Ayoub to clear the hell out of Yarda and try to join up with Haroun's men. It's all a gamble, for he's a coony old buzzard. He may not even listen or, doin' some deep figgerin', he may let on to do what I say and do something different." The gaunt sergeant shrugged. "Anyhow our outfit'll stand a better chance of polishing Ayoub off in the open country."

7

FORWARD TO DEATH!

THE DESERT WAS still very gray when from out of the battered gates of Yarda moved a long, irregular column of Touareg camel and horsemen.

So plausibly had Lemuel argued, pleaded and lied, that even the grizzled, tigerish Ayoub, more suspicious than suspicion itself, had become convinced of the deep and undying hatred Lemuel and his companion had for the Legion and all its works.

Perhaps the wily Shereef entertained ideas of making the captives into drill masters or, perhaps, he was reserving them for an orgy of torture at the end of the campaign. But anyhow the three white men now rode unbound and unarmed in the heart of the column. Though the weary three seemed quite forgotten by Ayoub and were ignored by the rest of the Forgotten of God, Lemuel was not for an instant deceived into thinking that they were not under close guard. Four Senegalese slaves, armed with nine-foot iron lances sharp as knitting needles, rode immediately behind the three white men.

Turmoil and racking anxiety raged in Lemuel's aching brain. Had he plotted aright in urging Ayoub to quit Yarda? What if Colonel Souchet, surmising his fate, had changed

his plan from that imparted to Captain Sedoux? What if
the powerful forces of Caïd Haroun, last reported by the
aviators to be seventy-five miles away, had defied Touareg
tradition and had marched all night? In that case the union
of the two commands would take place very shortly now
and the united forces, numbering five thousand, would
certainly prevail, despite any amount of desperate valor on
the part of the Legion.

'Arold's sparrow-like face, shaded by a tattered burnoose,
looked very worried in the pre-dawn light, and Obregon,
still numbed by his sufferings, rode a leaden weight on the
scrawny nag assigned to him.

All about Lemuel the terrain of yellow-gray clay and
rock was covered with a moving carpet of figures. Especially picturesque were the camelmen swaying high above
the horsemen.

Behind the departing *harka* the black, dawn-lit walls
of Yarda receded and soon the Touareg horde commenced
to travel swiftly, skirting rocky hillocks and a succession
of long, undulating hills, the valleys of which were strewn
with rocks deposited by a long departed ocean.

"Some scouting system," Lemuel muttered to 'Arold.
"But they don't send them flankers very far out."

"Yus," the cockney replied through chattering teeth,
"but we d-d-don't s-s-see 'alf of them. See that bloke 'way
over yonder?"

With a grimy forefinger he pointed to a scout who had
halted just below the skyline. The Touareg's camel, trained
with infinite patience, moved not a muscle and man and
mount might have been carved out of sandstone for all
their animation.

Very quickly Lemuel learned the organization of the Touareg forces. Under the Shereef were many vassal chieftains who, in turn, were followed by their own particular men-at-arms.

"Where in hell are the planes?" Lemuel grumbled. "They ought to be up by this time. How about it, *compadre?*"

A bluish bruise on Obregon's cheek made itself seen as he nodded.

"There was very little gasoline left last night, but I thought I heard motors a while ago. It's possible the flight's reconnoitering a line of retreat or perhaps they are busy bombing Ahmadu's camp."

IT WAS AROUND nine of the morning that the American sergeant's fading hopes suffered a sharp setback, for, galloping up amid a whirlwind of dust, a small cavalcade bearing a standard of green horsehair appeared from the desolate countryside to the east.

"Them will be some o' 'Aroun's blighters," muttered 'Arold, spitting dejectedly. " 'Im and old Ayoub will be joinin' the forces pretty soon now—Guess it's our necks.

"Now, wot the 'ell you rubberin' at?"

Lemuel had made no reply, but rode with lean head outthrust, his gaze fixed on that long rocky ridge off to the right.

"Look," he cried breathlessly. "See that?"

As the cockney's pale blue eyes turned they saw a scout, posted far out on the Touareg flank, reel and fall heavily from his saddle. Several seconds later the faint report of a rifle came winging over the desert.

"W'allah!" "The *Franzwazis!*" "*Allah Aleikoum!*"

At once the Touareg column halted and there descended

upon it a deep and disciplined silence as the other scouts came racing in, flogging their buff colored meharis with merciless energy.

The foremost flanker arriving before Shereef Ayoub saluted with his lance and reined in not twenty yards away from where the three prisoners sat their sorry steeds, all too aware that the machinery which would grind out their fate had already been set in motion.

The scout fortunately spoke in Arabic instead of Mahgreb, whereupon Obregon, who understood that language, gave close attention.

"Allah is kind and has delivered the unbelievers into our hands!" yelled the brown-featured scout. "The *Franzwazi* have split their forces! In the next *wadi* march less than twice a hundred of the accursed *Roumis*."

"Bismillah!" cried Ayoub. "We shall destroy them utterly and the jackals shall tear their bellies!"

A fierce murmur of pleasure burst from the blue-veiled captains, but a smothered groan rose from the depths of Lemuel's soul.

"So old Sowchay split the column! Of all the boob stunts!"

Bitterly he realized that all his careful plotting had gore for naught. As he had feared, Colonel Souchet had changed his plans—probably for the best of reasons; but the appalling fact remained that now the expedition, broken up into small detachments, would be wiped out in detail.

THE TRIBESMEN'S ATTACK took shape with a speed and efficiency that was highly complimentary to the Touareg leaders. In less than three minutes from receipt of the scout's report, the Shereef's two thousand men had fallen into a rough double rank with each detachment formed behind its lord and facing the long rocky ridge.

"Shows what these here soap-dodgers think o' the Legion," remarked Lemuel breathlessly apprehensive, "when they send two thousand men 'gainst less'n two hundred o' the boys—"

"To 'ell with compliments like that," growled the cockney, looking fearfully about. "You boggled it for fair this time, Lem Frost. If only old Ayoub 'ad stayed in Yarda—"

"Ah, shut up!" Lemuel was sensitive at this point.

"What will these devils do with us when they charge?" Obregon inquired.

" 'Pears like we'll go along with the charge." Lemuel gloomily reined in his horse and took the place indicated by a grinning Senegalese camelman. "Gawd, how I dread watching what's goin' to happen!"

And so, with a rare sense of irony, the Fates directed that the two Legionnaires should shortly face those deadly Legion volleys which they themselves had so often helped to deliver.

"Maybe we can get away during the fight," Obregon suggested, bruised features lighting hopefully.

But prompt evidence was had that the worthy Ayoub had foreseen just such a contingency, for, as he cantered by with his gold-trimmed burnoose blowing free, he called out: "Hearken, *Roumi* dogs! Be ye ever more than ten camel's lengths from my horse—then these," he nodded towards the Senegalese guards, "will dispatch ye to the flames of Eblis."

Slowly, the *harka* commenced to climb the long rock

and clay ridge which hid from view the doomed French force on the far side.

A silence broken only by the faint clink and clatter of equipment and the hoof beats of the nervous barbs fell over the gathering attack, a silence in which the dismayed sergeant heard, very faint and far away, the familiar shrilling of whistles calling in flankers.

Poor devils—in twenty minutes the lucky ones would be dead; the others—God help them!

Grimly alert, he kicked forward his mount—a sluggish beast purposely chosen to prevent a dash for escape. Meanwhile he tried to console himself with the thought that before long there would certainly be a number of good Touareg mounts with empty saddles to which he might switch if opportunity offered. It oughtn't to be hard for a veteran of the 4th U.S. Cavalry.

In an undertone he advised 'Arold and Obregon of his decision.

"If one of us can get away," he said, "we can warn the rest o' the column to concentrate in Agadés. Since Ayoub ain't got no artillery they can hold the place, maybe, until reënforcements come up."

There was no time for more talk. All about the prisoners, brown and black-faced warriors were making last preparations for the bloody work to come. One by one muskets, carbines and rifles were being unslung, lances were lowered to the charge position after certain of the Touaregs took heavy stone rings from their saddle pommels and slid them well up on their wiry arms in order to give their lance thrusts greater weight and power.

NOW THE BOWLDER studded crest of the ridge was nearly

reached and Lemuel saw the Shereef, his green-trimmed turban flashing bright, brandish his Gras carbine, turn in his saddle and raise that long drawn *"Ul-ul-ullah-Akbar!"* which torments the dreams of every Legionnaire who has fought a desert campaign in Africa.

With remarkable steadiness the double rank of horse and camelmen swept up to the crest and Lemuel's heart commenced to pound when the Touareg force took up a trot. Burnooses, djellabas and green horsehair standards commenced to flap and flutter. Faster, faster. The crest was almost reached.

"Yah! Il-il-Allahu Akbar!" And now Ayoub and his vassal chieftains dug heels into their charges and, on reaching the ridge crest, were momentarily outlined against the aching blueness of the African sky.

"Yah! Yah!" Terrible was the howling of the *harka* as it swept over the summit and a cold void was where Lemuel's stomach should have been when he caught his first glimpse of the doomed contingent. Considerably less than two hundred men were drawn up in a compact semicircle at the foot of a very sharp escarpment of yellow-red rock that rose sheer behind them.

Experience told Lemuel that this bluff was probably only one of several such faults and that another valley lay beyond the one which would in a moment become the scene of slaughter.

Subconsciously, he noted how very dark the Legion overcoats looked against the dazzling background. In that clear air every detail was sharp and distinct, revealing how pitifully few were the men in blue and white. As usual the front rank was kneeling, while the rear rank, with their bayonets twinkling like tiny diamonds, stood ready to fire over their heads. But they were hopelessly doomed, that Lemuel knew, for not even a hundred and fifty Legionnaires can beat off the determined charge of two thousand murderously inclined fanatics.

"*Yah! Ul-ul-ul!*" Faster and faster galloped the Touaregs and swirling clouds of dust veiled the slower camelmen who had already fallen behind. A Touareg, riding just in front of the tight-jawed sergeant, stood in his stirrups and fired, then another and another, until the little valley echoed and reëchoed.

With incredible speed the strip of heat-blasted earth separating the two forces narrowed. There was Ayoub, far out in front, brandishing his carbine and with his blue-black shadow showing sharp beneath him.

Then a gleam from the midst of that doomed semicircle caught the sickened sergeant's eye. It was the officer's sword being raised. Just then a bugle screamed a harsh, imperative call and on the bluff high above the doomed contingent a line of *képied* heads sprang into sight.

Cra-a-a-a! Another note was screamed from the brazen throat of that invisible bugle, only to be lost in the crashing volley that followed. Three hundred and fifty Lebels added their hail of lead to the first volley delivered by the decoy force in the valley.

CHAOS ENSUED; THE Touaregs, wholly surprised and well within range of the entire Legion force, gave no thought to flight and thundered on down the slope shrieking out their shrill war cries.

A camel fell heavily in front of Lemuel's horse, pitching its rider so that he tumbled over and over, like a duck shot in mid-air.

Louder swelled the battle, and bullets filled the air about Lemuel, who yelled in delight as the Touaregs commenced to go down in dusty, tangled heaps. Would they reach the sacrifice force?

Dust whirled high in the baking air and everything became confused, jerky, like a film that is run off too fast. Horses and camels, spears and flying robes eclipsed all else as, carried onwards by its own momentum, the charge swept on. Evenly the Legionnaires posted on the heights delivered one deadly volley after another. Saddles were empty all around Lemuel now, but he could not do anything but try to keep his feeble mount on its feet.

"Reckon I'll stop a slug in a minute," he reflected and commenced to laugh wildly. "Ha! Ha! Ha! Hell of a joke to get shot by the Legion after all!"

Then with surprising suddenness he glimpsed a ragged blue-white line just ahead. The surviving Legionnaires were firing desperately now, while dismounted Touaregs scrambled over a hideous, struggling barrier of dead and wounded to try conclusions with cold steel.

Frantically, the captive sergeant tried to rein aside. But it was no use, a frenzied Touareg on a racing camel was leading his followers straight on.

Dimly the crisp clicking of breech-locks came to Lemuel's ears above the indescribable tumult.

Hot dust filled his nose and eyes and his horse began to flounder and slip upon the dead which the animal could no longer avoid. Like a scene glimpsed by lightning, Lemuel sensed that row of *képied* heads less than thirty yards away.

Closer! Now he could see the wide eyes, the red panting mouths of the hard pressed Legionnaires. Now their heads bent over their light brown rifle stocks. The last volley would be delivered in an instant now.

"No! No!" he screamed, quite oblivious that his cry could no more be heard than the cheeping of a field mouse.

Just then a dying camel, madly threshing its ungainly legs, tripped the American's horse and he was flung violently into a heap of fallen Touaregs.

Half stunned, Lemuel remained where he fell, vaguely trying to dodge the lashing hoofs of a crippled stallion, and with his ears filled by the clash of steel.

8

COLD STEEL

"HELLO," REMARKED CORPORAL FAULKNER of the 7th Company, while tugging at the leg of an unmistakably dead Hausa, "there's a jolly big Touareg under the late lamented—and the beggar's still breathing, too."

"Bayonet or butt?" growled a huge Sicilian Legionnaire whose needle-like bayonet ran with blood.

"Bayonet," grunted the English corporal.

Taking care to make no sudden movements Lemuel, liberally splashed with the Negro's blood, opened his eyes and gasped, "Hold on, Bud, take it easy!"

"Talks English!" gasped the corporal. "Damned if it isn't a renegade."

"Renegade, my eye," rasped Lemuel, raising his lean head a little—it still swam sickeningly. "I'm Sergeant Lemuel Frost, 3rd Platoon o' the 6th Company."

"Bluffing will do you no good, my lad," snapped the corporal, a peculiar tight smile on his hot, bronzed face.

"But I am—"

In search of a familiar face, Lemuel looked past the menacing Sicilian and saw that the battlefield was largely deserted. Apparently the main column had moved on, leaving behind only a small detachment to dispose of the dead and wounded Touaregs. The sergeant promptly decided that Colonel Souchet had moved promptly on, with intent to fall upon Caïd Haroun, who must be still marching towards Yarda, quite unaware of the fact that the Shereef had fallen long since, his tough old body pierced by a dozen Lebel bullets.

"A sergeant of the Legion, eh?" Apparently Corporal Faulkner was going to be unpleasant. His heavy, not too intelligent features had assumed a forbidding expression. "—I *don't* think. What business has a sergeant of the Legion to be charging with a Touareg *harka?* No, my lad." He summoned three or four Legionnaires who searched cautiously among the fallen. "We know renegades when we see 'em. Hey, Tantorous, Schmidt, Valcour!"

They came running, red bayonets poised, for, in common with the rest of humanity, the Legion hates a renegade with a deep and an abiding hatred.

"No! No! Don't I—" Bloodied robes swaying, Lemuel tried to pull his leg from beneath his fallen horse.

"Lie still, you scum," rasped an evil-featured Legionnaire whose cheek had been laid open by a glancing lance thrust. "Lie still so I can *zigoullier* you proper. Come on, Hans, we'll make a real Christian out of him again. Put your bayonet through his right hand. Martinez, take the left."

They towered above the helpless sergeant, deadly hatred gleaming in their narrowed eyes.

"No, no!" yelled Lemuel. "Stop it, you damn fools!"

But, gleaming like falling stars, the bayonet points flashed downwards just as Lemuel, with a superhuman effort, squirmed sidewise. One of the bayonets, however, scraped his ribs before burying itself deep in the earth.

WHAT IRONY—TO HAVE successfully outwitted and led the Touaregs to their defeat; to have won Obregon's silence; only to perish at the last minute. If only these moppers-up had been men of the 6th Company! Making wild negative motions with his hands, Lemuel tried to recall the name of that captain who had sent him into Yarda.

" 'Tis like spearing an eel," remarked a bullet-headed Danish corporal. "Lie still, you treacherous dog, till we pin thee to the earth."

Eyes glazed with despair, Lemuel yelled out Sedoux's name.

"Sedoo knows me—Wait. Where's Capt'n Sedoo?"

Barely in time those murderous points were diverted.

"What's that?" snapped the English corporal. "D'you know the captain?"

"Oh, you fools!" Lemuel stormed as his hand tested the smarting wound on his left side—it felt as though a red-hot ax had hit him. Three inches to the right and he would have been cat meat—no mistake about it. "Corporal Hackbutt and me was sent into Yarda last night to spy. The A-rabs caught us and took us along. I lied us outta torture and steered the Shereef across your path."

Still deeply suspicious, the corporal briefly directed Lemuel to be freed from his fallen mount while the noise of a second engagement made the hot desert air quiver.

A brief search revealed 'Arold philosophically reclining under a dead Hausa and waiting for the moppers-up to reach him.

" 'Ello, cockey," he grinned up at Lemuel. "Fawncy finding you 'ere. I thought the boys 'ad dropped yer in that last volley."

"Jeeze, Bud," sighed the sergeant, vastly relieved, "it's sure a fact that the good die young—"

Flight Sergeant Obregon presently appeared and succeeded in making himself known just in time to avoid being shot from the saddle. The rescued captives found him standing among the Legion wounded and applying himself with remarkable concentration to a bottle of *Eau de Vie.*

"Ah!" Obregon's battered features lit. *"Dios de Dios*—I am glad you live, my friend! Now I can show my gratitude." With a fine flow of rhetoric he described to all and sundry the scene in the courtyard at Yarda. "So, *amigos,* it was Frost, here, who saved our lives. Saved your lives, too." He gazed around the ring of faces earnest and red-brown. "I suppose you all know what would have happened if Ayoub had sat tight in Yarda and let Haroun join him there?"

THERE FOLLOWED A significant pause in which the noise of the fight to the south swelled louder and louder.

"Looks like they're jolly well tangled with 'Aroun already," commented 'Arold. " 'Ere, let me get some Christian clothes. Guess this bloke won't object."

Methodically, and without the least intention of being callous, 'Arold squatted by the body of a Legionnaire about his own size and commenced to pull off his equipment and clothes.

"So you're Sergeant Frost, eh?" A black-bearded sergeant Lemuel had never seen before had come up to drop an armload of gold mounted knives and daggers onto an ever growing heap of weapons which were being collected by the moppers-up.

"Yes," said Frost, looking up quickly. There was something in the fellow's voice that sounded odd.

"How long you been away?"

"Since just after the alarm last night."

"Oh," the other sergeant shrugged, "then you've heard about that four thousand *franc* reward."

"Reward? For what?" Obregon momentarily checked a massage of shoulders which were still black and blue from the torment of the night before.

"Oh, haven't you heard?"

"I wouldn't be asking if I had."

"Well, Colonel Souchet's offered four thousand *francs* reward for information leading to the arrest of the two Legionnaires who started all the trouble by causing the death of Tchek Ahmadu."

"Four thousand *francs!*" Obregon smiled at Lemuel and nodded a little.

"Yeah," said Lemuel easily, "that's sure a lot o' mazuma, ain't it? Wish to hell I had a little of it."

'Arold's eyes sought those of his friend's and they were filled with keen anxiety.

"It is said a search and an investigation will be made," added Corporal Faulkner. "Some Fulahs think they can pick out the murderers—Damn them to hell!"

Obregon, his hands busy buttoning up the blood splashed tunic some one had handed to him, strode briskly over to Lemuel. "Never fear, *amigo,*" he said in an undertone, "from others he may find out, but with me your secret is safe. After what you did last night, not even four hundred thousand *francs* would tempt me—I will lie to save you."

The ring of truth was in the Chilean's voice and his

manner was convincing, so Lemuel breathed a little easier. But 'Arold thought otherwise.

"I told yer yer was wrong," he sniffed. "Should 'ave let the Toouaregs scupper 'im. 'Once a plug, always a plug,' says I."

9

COURT-MARTIAL

WHEN IN TURN Ahmadu's badly led forces had been taught to respect the mailed fist of *Madame la République,* Colonel Souchet remarked that "That was that," or words to that effect and ordered the weary column to return to Agadés.

"Gorblime, but 'asn't this been a day?"'Arold lay stretched on a dark blue blanket, noisily licking his fingers after having picked the last shreds of meat from a goat chop.

"Sure has; hope to hell I never see another like it!" sighed Lemuel, and, on gazing up into the starry heavens, he visualized a pair of lieutenant's *galons* among the blazing stars of the Milky Way.

He was feeling better pleased with the world—queer, but it sometimes paid to be a soft-hearted chump. If he hadn't shot to save Obregon from suffering, he'd never have been in a position to start Ayoub on the path to destruction.

He blinked lazily. Boy! Wouldn't it be nice to be an officer and gentleman again? Last time he'd held a commission was back there in Honduras.

"Ohé *la!* Sergeant Frost—Corporal 'Ackbutt."

" 'Ere come the medals," quoth 'Arold, and commenced

to do up the buttons of his dark blue tunic. "Fix yourself up nicely, Lemuel dear, and try to look like a tuppeny 'ero when they pins on the 'ardware."

Lemuel grinned and commenced to brush the dust from his sadly dirtied white trousers, then he glanced up and his sense of peace departed like a flea from a hot plate. Above him a sergeant was standing with a drawn pistol in his hand and an expression of great disgust decking his bronzed features.

"Steady, my brave, just leave that gun where it is. And you, the Englishman, raise your paws above your ugly head."

"Wot is it?" "What's wrong?" *"Qu'es-ce-qu'il-ya?"* "Leave them alone!" Voices about the bivouac fire commenced to call out.

"Silence—you misbegotten offal—this *bonhomme* is under arrest. Sergeant Frost and you, Corporal 'Ackbutt, I advise to come peaceably. Colonel Souchet's orders are to kill you if you make the least effort to escape."

"Nah then," snarled 'Arold while submitting to a search of his person, "yer can thank yer friend Obregon for this."

Lemuel said nothing, but the expression in his sunken gray blue eyes was terrible.

"FROM MY POSITION under the table," Obregon's deep voice quite filled the low ceilinged room, "I saw the sergeant, here, trip Tchek Ahmadu."

" 'E's lying, the dirty cad!" burst in 'Arold passionately. "Don't believe 'im! It was the lousy mucker's own foot wot tripped—"

"Silence!" Colonel Souchet brought his fist crashing

down on the greasy table behind which he sat together with the other officers of the court-martial.

"You are very sure it was Sergeant Frost?" Colonel Souchet's fine, war scarred head was thrust forward. "Think well—this is a vital matter."

"Yes, sir," the Chilean mumbled, and dropped his eyes, for the colonel's manner was forbidding as Death itself.

"That is all."

Lemuel, standing straight and silent between two guards, felt an immense weariness sweep over him. All for naught were the long years of faithful service in the Legion; gone for nothing were the appalling risks he and 'Arold had run the night before. And now he was to die because a mangy-souled traitor thought four thousand *francs* worth the price of betrayal.

Slowly, he studied the row of sunburnt faces behind that long table. By candlelight, the court-martial board looked infinitely severe and grim.

"Have you anything to say, sergeant, before the officers of the court deliberate upon the verdict?"

"No, sir. Nothing except I didn't trip Tchek Ahmadu."

"But you were at the Inn of the Three Moons?" Short and sharp, Colonel Souchet bit off every word, his gray mustache moving with tiny jerks. How his cold blue eyes bored into a fellow's soul.

"Yes, sir."

"And you were instrumental in causing the death of Tchek Ahmadu?"

The whole dimly lit little room seemed to spin about the gaunt American as he said in a low hopeless tone, "I reckon so. But please, sir," he held out an involuntary, pleading hand, "Corporal Hackbutt had nothing to do with it. He just happened to be along. He never touched the Tchek."

"That will do, sergeant."

On his camp stool Colonel Souchet, looking like a bronze figure clad in blue, turned to his colleagues.

"The case is so clear," he stated incisively, "that deliberation seems unnecessary. I shall ask you to think a moment, and then give me your verdict."

Lemuel stood as though carved from stone, chin up, eyes fixed straight ahead. Damned if he was going to make a show of himself, but before he died he'd give a hell of a lot to lay hands on that shifty-eyed swine across the room, for there was not the vaguest doubt in his mind as to what the verdict and the sentence would be. Briefly—"Guilty and Death." None knew better than Sergeant Lemuel Z. Frost that the Legion is very sensitive about military crimes committed in the face of the enemy.

COLONEL SOUCHET TURNED, a button sparkling briefly. "Gentlemen, your attention, please. Those of you who believe the prisoner guilty will please signify by raising their right hands."

Promptly all six of the court-martial officers raised their hands, and an unnatural, oppressive silence descended on the stuffy little room while Colonel Souchet very slowly got to his feet.

"Prisoner—attention!" The voice was as grim as the noise of earth dropping on the lid of a coffin. "Listen to the sentence of this court."

Lemuel stiffened and felt the perspiration breaking out on the backs of his hands.

"For being off bounds on the night of February 13th,

you are hereby sentenced to two weeks *salle de police;* for having caused the death of Tchek Ahmadu you are herewith recommended for the *Médaille Militaire.*"

Lemuel's gasp could be heard all over the room. What was the colonel saying? "—For further recognition for your valuable, devoted and intelligent espionage, you are herewith promoted to the grade of *Aspirant.* Corporal Hackbutt, incidentally, is recommended for the *Croix de Guerre.*"

In his heavy hobnailed shoes Lemuel swayed. What ghastly mockery was this? Damn them all! It wasn't fair to torture a man with death hanging low over his head.

"Wha—what's that, sir?"

Smiling, Colonel Souchet picked up several papers. "You are a little surprised, no? But we are very glad Tchek Ahmadu died when he did. Treacherously, our supposed ally was advancing upon our position. Only because he was killed did we order out patrols and so surprise him in the act of surprising us."

Amid a mad jumble of reaction, Lemuel recalled that unexpected and unexplained fighting which had broken out as his detachment had quitted Agadés. So that was it! The crowd he had fought was a part of Ahmadu's own men!

"One moment, gentlemen," Colonel Souchet's voice checked a general preparation to depart.

"Sergeant Obregon," he stated with an icy contempt, "it is an everlasting shame to France that such a vile creature as you has worn her uniform. But, nevertheless, France pays her just debts. Here—" Face frozen in disdain, the old aristocrat shoved a sheaf of blue and white bank notes across the table. "Take this four thousand *francs* together with the inexpressible contempt of this court-martial. Rest assured that a report of your infamous conduct will be made to your commander."

Utter silence prevailed while Obregon shambled miserably forward to pick up the notes with a trembling hand, and then prepared to take his departure.

"One moment, sergeant." Beneath his close-clipped gray mustache Colonel Souchet's lips tightened in a hard smile. "It has been brought to my attention that your quarters are—er—inadequate—therefore I have directed that you be quartered to-night in this room with Sergeant Frost. Guards, it is my order that no one but Sergeant Frost will be allowed to enter or leave this room to-night. Understand?"

"Yes, sir." The guards quite understood.

ABOUT THE AUTHOR

WORLD TRAVELER, ADVENTURER, Harvard graduate, and onetime liaison officer in the "A.E.F. is F.V.W. Mason.

He comes from a family of soldiers, a family steeped in martial tradition from the time they settled in this country three hundred years ago. When the Civil War broke over the nation seventeen of the Masons answered the call to arms. Two of them returned.

F.V.W. Mason began to read intensively in books of history and adventure when he was a small boy set back by a childhood disease. He started his travels early, in the days before the World War. His grandfather was a consul-general in Paris and Berlin and his family moved around Europe. When he was not traveling, he and his brother were in the woods hunting.

It was with his brother that he tried to get into the French Army when the Germans began their invasion. But both boys were 'way below the age limit. F.V.W. Mason waited two years and then managed to get overseas, first with the French and then as a lieutenant in the Interpreters' Corps of the American Army, in the capacity of a liaison officer. And he went through, over there, considerable action.

He came home after the war to get a degree at Harvard University. His summers he spent making land cruises from Marblehead to British Columbia and down the Pacific Coast to Mexico in a dilapidated flivver.

For a while after college he drifted—Central America and the Antilles, Hungary, Roumania and the other Eastern European countries.

It was the suggestion of a former instructor in English at Harvard that put him into writing. The instructor told him that stories he had written in college had always looked promising, and Mason decided to try his hand professionally. And he has been doing it ever since, with success that has borne out the teacher's prophecy.

www.ingramcontent.com/pod-product-compliance
Lightning Source LLC
Chambersburg PA
CBHW030543030726
47495CB00004B/1114